CW01108533

TAKE *it* EASY

DAVID HILL

MALLINSON RENDEL

*For Richie and Dave
and many river crossings*

ACKNOWLEDGEMENT
Publication of this book has been made possible by a grant from the Children's Publication Fund.

First published in 1995 by
Mallinson Rendel Publishers Ltd.
P.O. Box 9409, Wellington

© David Hill, 1995
ISBN 0-908783-04-3

Typeset by Wright & Carman Ltd, Upper Hutt, New Zealand
Printed by Colorcraft Ltd, Hong Kong

TAKE
it
EASY

One

SUNDAY: 11 JANUARY, 6.29am. On The Ground.

Their way out is blocked. Ahead, Rob can see the water roaring and pounding between great black rocks. They'll be smashed off their feet in there. There's no way round. They haven't the strength to go back.

SUNDAY: 11 JANUARY, 6.29 am. In The Air.

Victor Echo to Base: Dave, we've finished a sweep of the Awanui Gorge. Been down as far as the National Park Boundary. Still no sign of them. We'll try the ridges leading up to Hill 50. Over.

Base to Victor Echo: OK Tim. Victor Delta is just taking off to search the Boulder Stream and Nine-Mile Creek areas. Keep us posted. Over.

Victor Echo to Base: Will do. It's not looking good, Dave. Over.

Base to Victor Echo: I know, Tim. It's not looking good at all. Out.

MONDAY: 5 JANUARY, 10.00 am.

At last. Rob Kennedy tried not to sigh with relief as he heard his father get back in the car. Go, Rob begged silently. Please, just go. Then I won't have to feel ashamed of you.

At least on the drive up, his father had talked to him. That didn't happen much these days. After the road plunged into the cool, grey-green tunnel of trees that twisted and looped for nearly eighteen kilometres up to the National Park Lodge, he'd started making Rob go over the four basics of tramping safety—Keep Together; Sit And Wait If You're Lost; Leave Signs For Search Parties; Never Leave An Injured Person Alone. But by the time they reached the carpark, his father had fallen silent again.

A five-day Outdoor Pursuits tramp, right up to Wai-iti Saddle and Double Bend Station. Once, Ken Kennedy would have told stories to his son all the way from home to carpark.

True stories about doing the same trip when he was Rob's age. And way-out stories about the storm that tore a tree out of the ground beside Hope Hut, blew it over the hut roof, then rammed it so hard into the ground on the other side that it started growing again. Or how the track down to Awanui Gorge was once so steep that if you took your pack off and put it on the ground, it would slide all the way down the zigzag path to the bottom by itself.

Today his father didn't tell any stories. That was typical. He didn't really do anything now.

Three others—two girls (one wearing a Walkman) and a tall dark guy—were standing beside their packs in the carpark, talking to a grey-haired man in khaki shorts and shirt.

A car was just leaving, driven by a woman with a relieved expression on her face. Rob wondered if his father would look relieved too, when he drove away.

Then his father spoke suddenly. "Harvey Hall!" he exclaimed, looking at the grey-haired man. "Didn't think he was still taking tramping groups."

Harvey Hall grinned at them as they got out of the car. "G'day Ken. G'day young Rob. Glad you're coming Rob — wouldn't be a proper tramp without a Kennedy on it."

The other three stared at Rob. Then another car, a new red one, pulled into the carpark, and they started staring at the fair-haired girl getting out of it instead.

Rob's father turned back to him as Harvey moved over to greet the new arrival, who told him yes, she was Lara Foreman.

"I won't hang around, son," Ken Kennedy said. "You'll want to get your mind on the tramp."

Rob mumbled something, and pretended to be busy with the side pockets on his pack. Father and son were silent, not looking at each other. Harvey was introducing Lara to the others. Helen, Wiki, Carl were the names Rob heard.

"Have a great time, son." His father paused again. "Do us both good to be by ourselves for a bit. Remember those basics and take it easy, eh?"

Take it easy — Rob thought he'd scream if he heard those words again. He bent over his pack once more, in case his father tried to hug him. But the man just rested one hand on his shoulder and got back into the car.

Now, as he drove away, Rob lifted his head and stared after him. He turned around and saw that Harvey was also watching his father go.

Another car arrived. A woman dressed like a school-teacher got out. So did a short, wide boy with fair hair flopping over his eyes.

"Mr Hall?" the woman said. "I'm Beth Lander. This is Shawn Mills." The boy grunted.

"I'll see you on Friday afternoon then, Shawn," the woman added, after she'd helped lift an old blue pack out of the car. "Make the most of the experience, won't you?"

The boy pushed his hair out of his eyes, and grunted again. The woman looked at him for a moment, then drove off.

"OK, people," Harvey Hall announced. "Bring yourselves over and we'll get organised. The Great Escape begins right here."

The tall dark boy, Carl, dragged his pack across the asphalt. The others heaved theirs over to the Park Ranger.

Great Escape is right, thought Rob. And I'm escaping from my father.

Two

Tall dark Carl was Carl Chadwick. He was already looking at fair-haired Lara Foreman, who was already looking back at him.

Wiki Savage — "Don't worry, eh? I'm pretty tame really" — had the Walkman. Helen McLachlan was her long-legged friend. Shawn Mills kept his eyes on the ground and gave a couple more grunts.

"Hope you all followed the gear list we sent you," Harvey said when the introductions were over. "Cos 'm gonna check your packs right now. Nobody goes tramping without the right gear." Carl and Lara rolled their eyes wearily. Wiki took off her Walkman headphones and asked Helen what the guy had said.

"We'll start by leaving that behind, sorry." The Ranger pointed to the Walkman.

Wiki's face sagged. "Aw! You mean I've gotta spend five days with no decent music!"

"It'll save your batteries. Anyway, I don't want you getting lost because you can't hear us."

"Aw well," announced Wiki. "I'll just have to sing to you guys instead."

Helen sighed. "Shut up, Wiki. If you start singing, there'll be dead birds dropping out of the trees in all directions."

Wiki met Rob's gaze and winked. To his surprise, Rob found himself grinning.

Carl needed more plastic bags for his spare clothes, and a woolly hat. What did he need a woolly hat for in summer time? Because you lose half your body heat through your head, and it can get cold even in January where we're going, Harvey told him.

Helen needed better bootlaces. "Whaddaya been doin' with those?" Harvey demanded, as she undid her frayed laces. "Using them for dental floss!" the tall girl snapped.

Shawn didn't need the pack of cigarettes Harvey found inside Shawn's spare socks. Wiki's pack was so untidy, the Park Ranger couldn't tell whether she had anything missing or not. Lara was carrying deodorant and eyeshadow in her toilet bag. "You really need the extra weight?" Harvey joked. Lara pushed out her bottom lip, and stuffed the things back into a side pocket.

Inside the brown-timbered Park Lodge with its wall maps and photographic displays, they all wrote their names in the Intentions Book. Harvey had already entered the details of their tramp: 'Park HQ to Double Bend Station.

Track to Hope Hut, Off-Track by Boulder Stream, Nine-Mile Creek, Wai-iti Saddle. Four nights; arrive Double Bend Friday lunchtime.'

"Now Search and Rescue know where to drop my waterbed," the Ranger joked, as he pulled plastic bags, woolly hat and bootlaces from the Stores Cupboard.

Food ("But I've brought four cakes of chocolate!" said Wiki. "Or maybe it's five.") was shared out and packed. So were a primus stove and fuel refills. So were seven lightweight tent flies — one per person.

"Good track today," said Harvey. "No hurry — I'll lead to start with. Rob, you're pretty experienced; you go last." The others' heads turned towards Rob. Carl said something to Lara.

As they left the carpark, past the admiring gazes of a party of middle-aged tourists, Wiki was chattering to Helen. Carl, who swung his pack on to his back like an expert tramper when he saw the tourists, was talking to Lara. Even Shawn was replying with a few grunts to Harvey.

At the back of the line, Rob walked silently.

After ten minutes, the gravel path from the carpark turned into a dirt path and began sloping up into the instant quiet of the bush. The others became silent too. Breathing got heavier. Hands eased pack-straps into more comfortable positions. Boots stumbled occasionally where tree roots crossed the path.

Rob breathed slowly. He shortened his steps on the uphill bits and let his boots swing on the downhill bits, as his father had taught him. On the flat sections, he glanced up past cool trunks into the layers of different greens above. Crimson rata flowers blazed on high branches. The mid-morning sun sent white shafts smoking down through the trees. Rob felt a gentleness spreading inside him. His father would have loved this.

After an hour, Harvey called a break where the track curved around a clump of tall, grey-trunked trees. Packs were shrugged off gratefully. People folded with sighs on to the ground, found they were sitting on wet moss, got up muttering, and found stones to sit on.

Except for Carl. "You tired already?" he demanded.

"No hurry, remember?" Harvey told him. "Rush it in the morning, regret it in the afternoon. Five minutes break only — we'll get cold if we stop longer."

Wiki was passing around a cake of chocolate. "Come on, you guys; make my pack lighter, eh? Pity there's just us, else it'd go faster."

"It's a small group this summer," Harvey agreed. "We've tried to keep the cost down, but I guess people are finding the money harder to come by."

"My olds can afford it," Carl said quickly. "Even if they moan."

"My mother said it'll be good for my Geography work," said Lara, and tossed her long hair.

Wiki was already laughing. She dug an elbow in Helen's ribs. "Me and Helen won the tramp in a raffle! We went halves in a ticket at our School Gala!"

"So we only had to pay for half the tramp each," explained Helen. "I had to come — someone's gotta try and stop Wiki's noise pollution."

Eyes turned to Shawn, who was staring at his boots as he sat with legs stretched out in front of him. "Social Welfare paid for me," he grunted.

The others didn't know where to look for a few seconds. Then, as Rob knew would happen, they turned to him.

"Rob's been tramping for years," Harvey said, and Rob realised his father's friend was trying to help him. "His Mum and Dad had him carrying a pack when he was still in nappies." The Ranger stopped suddenly.

"Do your mother and father still go tramping?" Wiki asked.

"My father does a bit. My mother . . ." No matter how many times Rob spoke the words, they still sounded unreal. "My mother was killed three months ago."

Three

When they stood up to move on, Harvey stumbled on some loose stones and grabbed at the bank. "What'd you put in that chocolate, Wiki?"

The others laughed. Rob pretended to laugh, too. He owed people that much, after the way he'd upset them. When he'd said "three months ago", the words seemed to hang for a moment among the tall trees. Shawn lifted his head and looked at him. Wiki and Helen both opened their mouths to say something, then shut them. Carl and Lara stared into the distance.

Now the Park Ranger shrugged his shoulders into his pack straps. "Lunch in an hour, eh? Rob, you can go at the front now. Nice and easy, eh?"

Rob heard the echo of his father's words. He knew that Harvey didn't mean just the tramp.

Three months ago. In fact it was thirteen weeks ago tomorrow. Rob counted those weeks as he led the group around another ridgeside, above a riverbed where pale toitoi plumes stirred in the breeze. Thirteen weeks since a Tuesday in September.

The pictures formed again in his head. His Auntie Brenda's car had been parked outside their house when he'd got home from school. He remembered feeling pleased that his Mum's favourite sister was visiting.

But Auntie Brenda was crying when she met him in the front hall, while in the dining room his father was sitting at the table, hands in front of him, staring at the wall.

And somehow Rob knew straightaway what awful thing had happened. He knew it even though he tried not to know, even though he kept shaking his head, saying "Mum? Mum? *Mum?*" louder and louder, while Auntie Brenda held him and talked about the truck with its driver dazzled by the afternoon sun, and how the policewoman had told them that his mother wouldn't have known anything.

Finally it was his father who stood up, pulled him out of Auntie Brenda's arms into his own, and shook him hard, saying "She's dead, son. You have to hear me. She's dead!" Only then could Rob start crying.

He wasn't crying now, while the track began dropping towards the big boulder-bed of the Awanui Gorge. He hadn't cried for a fortnight, not since the time he'd seen something funny on TV, called out "Come and look at this, Mum!", and suddenly remembered.

His father didn't cry, either. He didn't do anything. He never went out, except to work, and to the supermarket when he remembered. At night he sat for hours and hours, staring at the TV without really watching it.

Rob would wake up when his watch said 1.15 am or 2.38 am, see the light shining under his door, and know that his father was still sitting in the living room alone.

Sometimes during the day, his father seemed suddenly to notice that Rob was there. He'd hug him, and talk, and even smile. Then he'd fade into being quiet again. Rob wanted to yell at him when this happened, bring him back from wherever he'd gone, make him do something, do *anything*.

When he was alone in his room, Rob would imitate the way his father sat — half-sloped forward, eyes staring at nothing. Hell, you look a dork! he'd tell his father, inside his head.

A couple of times, the anger he felt must have reached his father. "Easy, son," the man would murmur. "Take it easy." These were the words Rob hated most in all the world. He swore to himself that never, *never* would he give in to things like his father had.

He felt frightened about what was happening to his father now. That was another reason why he was pleased to get away.

They stopped for lunch in the Awanui Gorge. Wiki rummaged inside her pack, tossing crumpled T-shirts and shorts on to the ground. Then she passed her chocolate around again. "Come *on*! Jeez, I've still got three-and-a-half cakes to carry!"

People leaned against the big, sun-warmed boulders tumbled across the bed of the gorge, and ate their cut lunches. Helen took off her boots and spread her sweaty socks out on a rock to dry. "Hell, Chemical Warfare!" grunted Shawn, making his longest speech of the day.

"Takes a germ to smell a germ," Helen told him.

While they ate, and wriggled shoulders stiff from two hours of pack-straps, Harvey pointed up the wide, steep-walled gorge to where the mountains rose in shingle slides and stony ridges, shimmering in the January heat.

"The Dome," he said, naming peaks from right to left. "Kawahine. Hill 50. The Policeman. A day's rain on Kawahine, and you won't be able to cross this gorge for 48 hours. River tears through here with whole trees riding on it." The others looked at the water gurgling slow and soft among the rocks, and tried to imagine it.

"We're not going all the way up there, are we?" Lara shaded her eyes, and squinted towards the high slopes blue with distance, where bush thinned into scrub and tussock.

"No way," Harvey told her. "You don't want to be up on those mountains without extra gear, even in summer. Best views in the world. Most unreliable weather in the world. Nah, we'll stay down in the bush. Mightn't be able to see more than two trees ahead, but at least we won't get blown over any cliffs. OK, moving off in three minutes."

"Awww!" complained Lara. The others stretched and groaned, filled water bottles from the shallow water, put fresh sunblock on noses, retired modestly behind big rocks for a moment. "At least five metres from the river!" called Harvey. "Obvious reasons!" Carl looked embarrassed.

For the remaining hour-and-a-half to Hope Hut, Harvey put Helen in front. "Long legs like yours," he grinned, "you're the perfect choice."

"Perfect choice for what?" asked Helen. "A rake-handle?"

Rob went at the back again. He'd hardly spoken to anyone during the lunchbreak. They must reckon I'm a total drag, he decided. They're probably right.

Four

The sweaty seven reached Hope Hut in time for a late afternoon tea.

"My tongue's hanging out for a brew," Harvey announced, as a cheer from Wiki signalled the iron-roofed hut in its sunny clearing, big trees growing on *both* sides. "Tell you what, Lara—you get the primus going for a cuppa, and I'll let you off loading the dishwasher tonight."

"There's no dishwasher here!" Lara protested, after they'd left their boots on the back porch with its piles of cut firewood, and stepped into the stuffy hut. A couple of flies circled lazily, and an elderly tea-towel hung from the wooden drying-rack above the wood stove.

Carl was flicking the light switch just inside the door. "Bulb must have gone."

Harvey grinned. "Never been a bulb here, mate. Switch is just some Park Ranger's idea of a joke. Candles and torches only, sorry."

"Awww!" complained Lara again.

Deciding who would have which of the bunks with their battered foam-rubber mattresses took ten minutes. "Snorers sleep out on the porch," said Harvey.

Tea with condensed milk took twenty minutes. Searching for Wiki's chocolate took five minutes. "Now you know what a nuclear explosion looks like," announced Helen, as they watched Wiki stuffing gear back into her pack.

Comparing sore shoulders from straps and sore knees

from steps took quarter of an hour. Comparing feelings about the corrugated-iron long-drop loo, standing like a cross between a giant letterbox and a tiny bus-shelter on the far side of the clearing took another quarter of an hour. ("Gross!" said Lara. "Unbelievable!" said Carl. "Grunt!" said Shawn. "Spiders!" said Wiki.) And suddenly it was time for dinner.

"You always share the work when you're tramping," Harvey told them. "So three of you can cook dinner, and the other three can do the dishes."

"How about you?" protested Wiki.

"He'll do the eating, of course," said Helen.

Carl and Lara spent most of the time talking to each other while they boiled, mixed and stirred the rice, mince and peas. Rob didn't mind — it was pretty obvious already that Carl thought fair-haired Lara was the only person worth paying attention to on the tramp, and that Lara thought the same about dark-haired Carl.

Rob also knew that they didn't know what to say to him, because of his mother. The same thing had happened with his friends back home. At first when they weren't sure how to talk to him, Rob felt special. Then, when his friends chatted and laughed to one another instead, he felt alone and left out. It was the same now with Lara and Carl.

After dinner, the others sat around Hope Hut's old wooden table, with names and initials carved all over its surface, and played cards. Wiki didn't play. Instead she sat beside Shawn and told him exactly which cards to put down.

Rob didn't play either. He folded his spare clothes inside his sleeping-bag cover for a pillow. He put on a jersey. Then he wandered back along the track for fifty metres to where a tiny creek, hardly deep enough to wet the bottoms of his boots, whispered over gravel and stones.

He sat on a rock, watching a far-off ridge glow orange as the sun dipped towards it. A speck which must be a late-hunting hawk was wheeling above. Rob wondered if his father was staring into the TV at home.

A scuff of boots on stones made him look round. The squat shape of Shawn was approaching.

"Who won the card game?" Rob asked.

"Huh!" Shawn sat on another rock near Rob. "Whassername—Wiki—she kept giving me all these orders, so I told her she'd better play instead of me. So she takes my cards, gives me a bit of chocolate, and tells me to go see if I can find some Kentucky Fried."

Rob laughed. "She's all right."

The other boy grunted. "Yeah, I know. So's that friend of hers—the murder-mouth one. But don't tell her I said so, eh?"

He pulled a leaf from a nearby shrub, chewed it, then threw it away. "Hell, I could do with a smoke!"

"You should've brought two packets," Rob said. "Harvey would probably have stopped looking after the first one."

Shawn grunted. The two boys sat in silence. The distant ridge began turning from orange to purple as the sun slid behind it.

"Sorry about your mother," Shawn said suddenly.

Rob stared at the lichen growing grey and orange across the rock beside him. "I didn't mean to make a big thing of it. It just came out that way."

"People dunno what to say, do they?" Shawn was quiet again for a few seconds. Then, "At least you know what happened to your mother. That's something."

He stood up. "Jeez, I'd kill for a smoke. See ya back at the hut."

Rob sat on. The bush around him fell silent as darkness grew. From behind the far ridge, a final spear of sunlight struck upwards. The speck which was the day's last hawk turned gold, circled again, then sank from sight. In total silence, Rob began to cry.

Five

SUNDAY: 11 JANUARY, 7.44 am. On The Ground.

Rob can see the next hold in front of him. He only has to reach out and he's safe. But he can't do it. His arm won't move. His body is tight with terror. He's going to fall.

SUNDAY: 11 JANUARY, 7.44 am. In The Air.

Victor Delta to Base: Dave, there's nothing in the Boulder Stream or Nine-Mile Creek area. Over.

Base to Victor Delta: OK Phil. We should be hearing from Blue ground party soon. They've gone in to check Rata Hut, in case someone ended up there. I'll let you know as soon as we hear from them. Over.

Victor Delta to Base: Ken says he can't believe they'd go that way. Over.

Base to Victor Delta: Yeah, I know, Phil. But tell Ken we've gotta try everything we can think of now. Out.

TUESDAY: 6 JANUARY, 7.10 am.

"The exciting bit starts today." Harvey spoke through a mouthful of breakfast muesli. He paused to spoon some powdered milk from his chin, and went on. "No more huts. We'll make shelters with the fly-sheets for the next three nights. And no more tracks—just the map and compass."
 The Park Ranger paused. "You guys taking all this in?" Lara yawned. Carl rubbed his eyes. Helen and Rob propped their chins in their palms and looked blank. Shawn scratched his head. Even Wiki was quiet.
 "What's the matter with you lot?" Harvey demanded. "You look like a Zombies' Picnic."
 "We couldn't sleep!" said Lara.
 "You snored!" said Carl.
 "All night!" said Rob.
 "Like a jumbo jet!" said Helen.
 "Thought snorers slept in the porch," said Shawn.
 "Threw two cakes of chocolate at you," said Wiki.
 "Dunno what you're moaning about," said Harvey. "I never heard a thing."

Outside Hope Hut, the morning air smelled as if someone had just washed it in freshly-running water. The six non-sleepers took deep breaths and felt their eyes creak open.
 "Remember—we're off-track, so we go *very* slowly," Harvey told them. "Close together, single file, and you keep checking the person ahead and behind you. If you can't see them, call out. Anyone calls out, everyone stops."
 "We'll take all day getting there," Carl grumbled.
 "Get lost from your party in the bush, and you might take all *month* getting there." The joking had gone from Harvey's voice. "Like I say—slowly!"

The morning was very slow indeed, for a fairly experienced tramper like Rob, anyway. Harvey gave his party plenty of chance to get used to moving through the bush, in the cool green shade where the sky was just an occasional blue glimpse above, where trees and logs and ferns and slopes meant that the world shrank to a ten-metre circle.

Rob was at the back again. Shawn was in front of him, and every couple of minutes the thick-set boy would turn, check Rob was there, push his floppy hair from his eyes, and move on again. A couple of times he and Rob exchanged grunts. Mostly they said nothing. Rob didn't mind. Shawn was OK.

So was Wiki, talking and laughing two places ahead. "We don't need an Emergency Locator Beacon," Helen called back once. "Just leave the Savage signal switched on."

The sharp-tongued Helen was OK, too. As for Carl and Lara — well, they were too wrapped up in themselves to take notice of anyone else. Rob could handle them.

He'd decided while he lay in his sleeping bag last night, listening to Harvey's snores shake the hut, that he was going to handle things. He wasn't going to do nothing, like his father. He'd show people that he didn't just sit around when things went wrong.

"Wouldn't want to be lost in here, boy," Wiki declared when they stopped for their first rest after lunch. "Anyone know where we are, apart from Big Chief Thunder Snore here?"

There were head-shakings from the others, Rob included. He'd never been this way before.

"I don't know where we are, either," Harvey announced. The others stared at him. "Oh, great!" muttered Lara. Rob, who guessed what was coming, said nothing.

"Actually, I don't know *exactly* where we are," Harvey said. "But the map and the compass tell me which way we should be heading. And the map also tells me — come on, come here and look — that we have to cross Boulder Creek." The Ranger's finger pointed to a blue wriggle on the map. "So as soon as we fall in the creek, we'll be right. Should be about half an hour away."

In fact, it was only another twenty minutes till the slope they were climbing reached the top and angled down towards a glimpse of shingle and a murmur of water.

"Race ya!" Carl began striding down the steep bank, grabbing for handholds on branches and trees as he went.

"Wait!" Harvey's command stopped the tall dark boy in mid-stride. He stared back up at the Ranger.

"Aw, come on! Thought this was supposed to be an adventure."

Harvey's voice was level. "I know you're a fit young guy, Carl, but you fall and break an ankle, and this isn't an adventure; it's an emergency. I don't want to have to follow the river down for two days, till I find some farm with a telephone. Now go carefully."

The next time Shawn looked back to check on Rob, he dropped one eyelid in a wink. Carl meanwhile sulked all the way down to Boulder Creek, across the narrow bed, and through the next hour-and-a-half till Harvey called a halt to make camp.

Six

"Always give yourself plenty of time when you're putting up a shelter," Harvey said. "No fun trying to set up camp in the dark."

The others were clearing branches and twigs and dirt lumps from the clearing where a tree had grown up, grown old, and toppled over into the other trees. Shawn, who Rob noticed was paying more and more attention to Helen, had just dangled a dead weta in front of her nose.

"Didn't know you had relatives here," Helen told him.

Four tent flies were spread flat. ("Always get as much under you as you can. Otherwise all your body heat goes into the ground.") Three others were tied to branches and logs so they made a low roof. With their sleeping bags spread out inside, it all looked very cosy—except for the part where Wiki's sleeping bag and gear lay crumpled; it looked very messy.

"Sure you wouldn't like a little tent to yourself, Harvey?" Helen suggested meanwhile. "About twenty k's away?"

"See that dead branch caught up in the other trees there?" Harvey pointed. The Primus had heated them a cup of tea, and they'd fought off Wiki's offer of chocolate. "If we had a monkey in the party, we could get it down and have a campfire."

"I'll have a go," Shawn said. Behind Shawn's back, Carl did chimpanzee scratchings with his arms, then smirked at Lara.

"Push with your legs . . . hands just for grips . . . keep three points of contact . . . don't look down . . . you've done this before!" called Harvey, as the thickset figure worked its way steadily up towards the dead branch.

"Social Welfare sent me on a Rock-Climbing Course," a voice grunted from above. "Look out—timber!"

Dinner was over. Coffee was made, with water from the tiny stream that filtered down a fern-filled gulley towards Boulder Creek. The campfire blazed up. The stars shone down.

"This is cool!" announced Wiki. "Wish Mum and Dad were here to do the dishes, though."

She caught Rob's eye, stopped, and bit her lip. *It's OK, Rob* found himself wanting to say to her. *It doesn't matter.*

"Long-range forecast said another fine day or two ahead. Might get a drop of rain to finish with." Harvey stretched.

Around the fire, talk came easily. Wiki described how she used to help with a Church Youth Group, and how she got into trouble for telling one kid he was a real little devil. Carl told how he wanted to join the Army. Lara suddenly said she was always nervous when she was with people for the first time.

Harvey told a couple of stories about tramping trips with Rob's father "when I was young and Ken was younger", and how a plastic bag of sugar and coffee inside Harvey's sleeping bag had come open. "Rob's Dad reckoned we should just pour hot water into my sleeping bag. That way I'd have coffee in bed."

Later, when they were getting into their own sleeping bags and arguing over who could go furthest away from Harvey, the Ranger said quietly to Rob, "Your Dad'll come right, Rob. Just give him time."

Then, while Rob thought of ten things to say, and said none of them, Harvey yawned. A gold filling glinted in his lower jaw. "Jeez, it's hard work, baby-sitting you lot. I'm stuffed. Bring us a cup of tea and three doughnuts in the morning, Wiki."

Rob woke twice in the night. The first time, the embers of the campfire were still glowing dully. A morepork called from the bush, and Helen or Lara murmured something without waking. Everything else was quiet; on one side of him, Harvey lay without snoring.

Out past the edge of the tent fly, two stars shone white through the tree tops. Rob felt the same gentleness that he'd felt on the first day, looking up to the sunlight and the rata flowers. Yeah, he thought. Harvey's right. Dad just needs time. I'll try and be more patient when I get back.

The second time he woke, even the morepork was silent. On Rob's other side, Shawn turned in his sleep and sighed. The same two stars shone. Man, I'm enjoying this sleep, Rob told himself as he drifted off again.

Seven

SUNDAY: 11 JANUARY, 10.25 am. On The Ground.

Pictures keep coming. Pictures of the two bodies lying there. One in a clearing; one beneath a cliff. It's your fault, a voice is telling him over and over. It's all your fault.

SUNDAY: 11 JANUARY, 10.25 am. In The Air.

Base to Victor Delta: Come in Phil. Over.

Victor Delta to Base: Go ahead Dave. Over.

Base to Victor Delta: Phil, tell Ken that we'd like you back here now. We'd better have another briefing about things. Blue ground party found nothing at Rata Hut. Over.

Victor Delta to Base: Dave, Ken says he wants to keep looking. Over.

Base to Victor Delta: I know how he's feeling, Phil. But we want both choppers back here. We've got to try and come up with something new. Out.

WEDNESDAY: 7 JANUARY, 6.50 am.

A hissing sound and a giggle brought Rob up into the bright yellow-and-blue of a fine morning. The hissing sound was the Primus that Helen and Wiki had going. The giggle — of course — was Wiki.

"Hiya," she grinned as Rob raised his head. "Want a bit of chocolate?"

Rob shuddered and refused politely. He exchanged grunts with Shawn, who was lying on his back watching the sunlight creep across a corner of the tent fly above. Lara and Carl were stirring and yawning. Harvey slept silently on; his grey hair and one ear showed above the pulled-up sleeping bag.

"Maybe he only snores in huts," said Shawn, jerking his head towards the Ranger.

Five minutes later, the Primus had boiled. Carl and Lara had both combed their hair, everyone had refused Wiki's offer of chocolate, and Helen was pouring seven mugs of tea and condensed milk. Only Harvey hadn't moved.

"Time our guide woke up," said Carl.

"Yeah," agreed Lara. "Thought our guide was supposed to be guiding us."

"I'll give him some tea." Helen took a mug, bent her long legs while Shawn watched admiringly, and began working her way towards the far side of the tent fly where Harvey lay.

"Hold it under his nose!" called Wiki. "That'll wake him up."

"I'll stick it up *your* nose!" Helen replied. "That might *shut* you up!"

"Hope Harvey knows where we're going today," muttered Lara, hands clasped around her tea. "I haven't a clue where we are."

"I think we're—" Rob began. He stopped as a noise came from behind them.

Helen was kneeling by Harvey's sleeping bag. Her hands were up to her face, and she was making ragged gasping noises. The mug of tea had fallen on its side, pooling across the tent flies folded on the ground.

Harvey still lay unmoving. But now they could see him, where Helen had lifted back a fold of the sleeping bag. His face was white. His mouth hung slightly open, and Rob saw the gold filling again. His eyes were open too, staring straight ahead.

"He—" gasped Helen. "He's dead!"

Eight

Ten minutes later, Helen crouched at the corner of the tent-fly shelter furthest from Harvey's body, with Wiki holding her. There was no sign of the tall girl's sharp tongue now. Sobs and shudders still shook her.

Lara and Carl stood staring into the dead ashes of last night's campfire. They both held mugs of tea in their hands, but the tea was nearly cold. Once, Carl lifted his mug and took a sip. Then he looked guilty, glanced around to see if anyone was watching, and lowered the mug.

While Wiki rushed to Helen, put her arms around her and led the shaking girl away, Rob and Shawn Mills stared at each other. Shawn had a dirt smear across his forehead where he'd wiped a sweaty hand yesterday afternoon.

Then, stooped over beneath the tent-fly roof, Shawn made his way across the scatter of packs and sleeping bags to where Harvey lay, eyes staring ahead. He squatted down, reached a hand out slowly, shivered, then rested it on their guide's forehead.

"Harvey?" he said. "Harvey?" Then, as Rob joined him, "He's cold." There were more gasps from the others.

Rob thought of the Bush Safety Courses his father had taught. He also reached out, shivered like Shawn had done as his hand approached the pale, still face, then made himself lay two fingers behind Harvey's cheekbone, just under his ear. The skin felt clammy; the big carotid artery was slack under his touch.

He straightened up, exchanged glances with Shawn, then

looked across to where the others stood or knelt, staring at him. He nodded once. Helen burst into tears again and Wiki held her tighter. Lara whimpered "Oh no!" Carl stared at the ground.

Then Shawn gently pulled the corners of the Park Ranger's sleeping bag up over his face. As the two boys stood up, so did Wiki. "Hey, Lara. Come and give Helen a hug, eh? You look like you could do with one yourself."

Lara came across, looked awkward for a moment, then sat and put her arms around the still-shaking Helen's shoulders. "I wish I hadn't said all those smart-arse things to him," Rob heard Helen mumble.

Wiki meanwhile moved over to where Harvey lay. She knelt, placed a hand on his shoulder, and began murmuring in Maori.

As she murmured, she lifted her hand slowly from the guide's body, up towards the morning sunlight now glittering in the treetops, spread her fingers wide, and slowly lowered her hand.

Then Wiki stood again, came back to the others, and without saying a word, hugged them one after the other. "OK," she said. "What are we gonna do now?"

Nine

What they did was to make more cups of tea.

"I can't!" exclaimed Lara, when Rob moved to light the Primus again. "Not now!" And Carl, who'd followed Lara across to Helen, shot Rob an angry look.

"It's now you need it." Rob remembered his father's Bush Safety Courses. "We all need it. We're all in shock. First thing to do is to sit down and take it easy." He stopped as he heard his own final words.

Shawn grunted agreement. "I reckon."

Helen stood up. She took a handkerchief from the pocket of her shorts, wiped her eyes and blew her nose. "I'll make the tea. Hell, I've howled enough to fill three mugs! Thanks, everyone; I feel much better now." She began to smile shakily at the other five, and burst into tears again.

But Helen made the tea and they all drank it, even Lara. Wiki passed around more of her chocolate, with no jokes this time. Carl and Lara hesitated, but when they saw the others eating, they did, too. Everyone stood by the campfire ashes, backs turned to Harvey's body.

When Shawn finished his chocolate, he looked around for a moment, picked up a twig, and started chewing the end of it. "Next time I'll bring *three* packets of smokes," he muttered. The others half-laughed, and suddenly they seemed able to move and talk properly again. "Who wants more tea?" Helen asked, and began pouring without waiting for an answer. The tall girl was still pale, but her hands were steady.

Shawn spoke again. "What are we gonna do about Harvey?"

Carl stared at him. "How do you mean?"

"What about his—his body?" Shawn hesitated, then went on. "We can't just leave it there, where we'll see it all the time."

"We're not staying here, are we?" Lara's voice went high and shrill. "I can't! Not with him!"

"We've got to go," Carl agreed. "Get help."

Rob thought of the four safety basics his father had gone over with him. "We should stay here till they search for us."

"Sit around on our bums and do nothing?" Carl's sneer at Rob was the sneer Rob knew he'd given his own father. "No way!"

"Let's keep going to that place—Double Bend Station." Lara's voice was still high. "They can come back and—and fix him." She half-turned towards Harvey's body, then quickly turned back again.

Shawn took the twig from his mouth. "Harvey said you and your old man have done a fair bit of tramping, Rob. You reckon we should stay here?"

All eyes turned to Rob. He swallowed.

"Search and Rescue say that if you're lost in the bush, then you sit and wait. Do anything you can to make signs, but stay put till they find you."

"We're not lost! Search and Rescue!" Lara and Carl burst out together.

Helen sighed, and some of the sharpness came back into her voice. "You two know where we are? Know how to get to Double Bend Station?" Silence from Carl and Lara.

"Go on, Rob," said Shawn. Rob did, more confidently.

"We're supposed to reach the Station the day after tomorrow. Search and Rescue won't start doing anything till that night. We filled in the Intentions Book back at the Lodge, so they know roughly where we're going. We should stay here. Keep safe, and make signs for them."

"What signs?" Carl demanded. "You can't see further than the next bloody tree in here! Who's gonna see any signs?"

Rob pointed around the little clearing where the old tree

had fallen. "We make a fire. We keep it going all the time—flames at night; leaves and stuff for smoke in the day. Search and Rescue will do an air search, and they'll put in ground parties from each end. They'll try the area we're supposed to be going, all the huts anywhere near, plus any known danger spots."

Rob found himself getting quite carried away by what he was saying. "Dad says they even look in the rubbish tins for any paper or stuff that shows we've been there. And they check the long-drops too."

"Aw, yuk!" Wiki protested.

"No point in starting the fire yet, I guess," grunted Shawn. "Nobody's gonna be looking for a while."

"I'm not staying where there's someone dead!" Lara's voice was even shriller than before.

To Rob's surprise, it was Helen who moved across and put an arm around the frightened girl. "It's OK, Lara. We're not gonna leave him there."

"Helen's right—for once." Wiki forced a grin of sorts on to her face. "Come on, people. Let's sort it out."

Moving Harvey took five of them nearly an hour. Lara refused to come near; refused even to watch the others while they struggled.

It was almost impossible to get a grip on the heavy body as it sagged inside the sleeping bag. Nobody wanted to hold the dead man's head. Finally, Rob and Shawn each gripped the sleeping bag's top, trying not to let the white face fall against their hands. Carl and Wiki took the middle. Helen had the feet. Together they half-lifted, half-dragged the clumsy weight across the clearing. They stumbled and clambered over roots, logs and fern clumps to the tall totara tree Wiki had chosen, and laid Harvey beside it, on a folded tent fly.

Wiki pulled the sleeping bag over their guide's face again. Shawn and Rob and Helen spread another tent-fly over him, weighing it at the corners with his pack and pieces of moss-covered logs.

"Wait," said Wiki as they turned to go, and while the others stood awkwardly by, she knelt at the head of the wrapped shape, and murmured softly in Maori once more.

Then they went back into the half-clearing where Lara was waiting.

That night, Rob lay on his back, staring out under the tent fly at the same two stars he'd watched the night before. They glittered in and out of thin fingers of cloud that had spread across part of the sky.

Beside him the others lay awake or slept briefly, jerking in and out of dreams. Nobody spoke. Nobody had spoken much during the rest of the day. A couple of times Rob heard someone — Lara, he thought — crying, and trying to hide the sound inside her sleeping bag.

Weird, he thought as he finally slipped into a doze. I was so angry at Dad for just sitting there and doing nothing after Mum was killed. Now I'm telling people to do exactly the same.

Ten

SUNDAY: 11 JANUARY, 11.30 am. On The Ground.

The noise is getting fainter. Rob knows that every step is leading him further away. He's got to get back to the river; there's no way out except the river.

SUNDAY: 11 JANUARY, 11.30 am. In The Air.

Victor Echo to Base: Over.

Base to Victor Echo: Come in Tim. Over.

Victor Echo to Base: We can see Red ground party at Hope Hut, Dave. We're gonna sweep the scrub line along the top of the bush now. Can't really imagine Harvey taking anybody up there, though. Over.

Base to Victor Echo: Me neither, Tim. Still, we've tried just about everything else. Keep us posted. Out.

THURSDAY: 8 JANUARY, 7.11 am.

When Rob came awake next morning, to hear the Primus hissing and voices murmuring, it was a few seconds before he remembered about Harvey. Then he sat up quickly, feeling ashamed of sleeping in.

Helen gave him a strained smile. "Hiya, Sleeping Beauty. Sleeping Ugly, I mean."

Rob smiled back. Having Helen back to her quick-tongued self somehow made things feel better.

Most of them drank their tea still lying in their sleeping bags. There was no point getting up when they were only passing time till a search started. Anyway, the morning was cool; a haze of high cloud could be glimpsed through the treetops, and a wind was stirring the branches.

"Nobody got a cellphone, have they?" Wiki asked suddenly.

There were blank looks from the others.

"Well, you hear how some dudes get lost in the bush; they ring up on their cellphone and say, 'I'm lost; send a taxi'. Just thought I'd ask."

Nobody had a cellphone. There was a pause. Then Helen began, "I've been thinking—"

"Thought I heard a creaking noise," Shawn interrupted, and winked at the tall girl. There were grins from a couple of others. Shawn's a useful guy to have around, Rob decided.

Helen pulled a face at Shawn. "Didn't think you could hear anything, with all that concrete between your ears." She started again. "I've been thinking, we'd better see how much we've got to eat. If we have to wait till someone comes looking for us, we could get short of food. Maybe we should measure it out."

The others nodded. "Cool! Now I can get rid of that chocolate," said Wiki.

There were no smiles; Helen's suggestion made things seem a lot more serious.

"We're carrying food for two more days. Rob reckons the search should start in three days. I reckon we should try to spread things over four days."

Helen was looking at the packets and plastic bags now lying in the middle of the sleeping area. Quickly and neatly, she began sorting the pile into four smaller piles.

"That's not much for a day!" protested Lara. Carl muttered agreement.

"Better to be hungry than have nothing," Rob said. "Anyway, if we're just sitting and waiting, we won't need so much energy." He added something his father had told him. "We'll survive—as long as you've got water, you can go for a week or more without food."

Carl sneered. "Know it all, don't you? Sitting on our bums, not even trying to help ourselves. Hell, can't we do better than that?"

Awkward silence for a few seconds. Then Shawn grunted, "Rob's right. We stay put."

Rob said nothing. There was going to be more bad temper before this was over. And anyhow, he recognised in Carl's words the things he'd so often said to himself at home.

They ate a very small breakfast of muesli. "Have it with lots of water," said Rob, ignoring Carl's glare. "It'll fill up your stomach more."

After breakfast, Wiki and Helen began collecting twigs, half-dry ferns, fallen branches — anything to make the fire they'd decided to start later that day.

"No talking till Saturday, Wiki Savage," the tall girl ordered. "Then the search parties can home in on you from ten k's away."

Lara and Carl started picking up dishes and waterbottles to wash and fill in the little stream — where they could have a private moan, Rob suspected. Rob and Shawn began heaving and hauling at a big wet log lying a few metres into the bush.

"That'll never burn!" Lara pushed back her hair, which the growing wind was blowing across her face.

"It's not for the fire. We're going to lay out a signal on the ground by the fire, so if a chopper sees us, they'll know we need help."

"How?" Carl was standing with hands on hips, not offering to help.

"We lay logs out in a V and an X. V means we need help. X means we need a medic. It's Search and Rescue Code all over the world."

Lara and Carl said nothing. After a few seconds, they moved off.

Rob and Shawn wrestled the first log into the half-clearing. They straightened up to get their breath back. Rob, not looking at the other boy, suddenly said, "Shawn? You know what you were saying at Hope Hut, how at least I knew my mother? It's none of my business, but—"

Shawn gazed at the bush. "It's OK. Nothing to tell, really. My Mum was into drugs real heavy. Social Welfare took me away from her when I was four. She's never tried to get in touch, far as I know." Shawn shrugged. "That's about it."

And I thought I had things tough, Rob told himself. He turned towards Shawn. "I'm sor—"

Like a wet towel slapping concrete, a gunshot sounded in the bush further up the slope from the clearing. A noise that could have been a voice calling came faintly on the wind.

Wiki and Helen burst out of the trees on the other side, half-falling over their own firewood pile. Yells and crashings came from down the slope, where Lara and Carl were returning with the dishes and waterbottles.

"Must be a hunter!" Rob said. "Two of them, maybe." He called to Carl and Lara as they came into view. "Hunters!"

Carl began yelling into the trees at the top of his voice.

"Someone's found us!" exclaimed Lara. "We're going to be all right!"

Eleven

The next five minutes were madness.

"Here!" Carl had his hands cupped around his mouth, yelling as hard as he could towards where the shots had come from. "Over here!"

Lara joined in, her voice high and thin in the wind. She and Carl stopped as a second shot sounded. "They haven't heard," Helen muttered.

Lara shouted again. A surge of wind in the trees rushed over her voice. "Wind's blowing the wrong way." Shawn was totally still, listening. "It's coming from where they are. We can hear them; they can't hear us."

"Light the fire!" Carl scrambled towards the pile of wood on the clearing's edge. "Light the fire!"

Helen fumbled for the matches. Carl and Lara searched frantically for dry wood. Wiki dived for the bags of food, tore a block of her chocolate from its wrappings, and crumpled the paper.

Helen's first match went out in the wind. The second snapped as she struck it.

"Here! Give them to me!" Lara snatched at the box, knocking the matches on to the ground. She grabbed one, struck it, and lit Wiki's chocolate paper while Rob sheltered the flames with his cupped hands. Wiki thrust the flaming paper into the pile of twigs Carl had hastily made.

"Burn! Please burn!" urged Lara. The paper sputtered, flared and went out. Carl tore it from the twigs, hissing "Hurry! Hurry!" as Lara struck another match, then

pushed it back under. Once again the chocolate wrapping flamed. The twigs above it began to smoke. Then as the paper burned out, the tiny white wisps thinned and faded away.
"You need time to build a proper fire." Shawn Mills' voice was flat. "It's no use." Even as he spoke, a third shot came, faint and distant.
Lara threw the matches on the ground and turned away. Carl kicked the pile of twigs so it scattered across the clearing. Then he whirled on Rob.
"Useless bloody dork!" he stormed. "Sit here and wait, you reckon. If we'd got moving, we might have walked into those guys. We might be on our way home now!"
"Take it —" Shawn began. Carl turned on him.
"Don't you tell me to take it easy! *I'll* tell *you* something! I'm not gonna just sit around any longer. I'm gonna find a way out of here, whether you're coming or not!"

Twelve

Wiki tried to calm Carl down. "Look, maybe we would have run into those hunters. Maybe we should do something. But let's work it out, eh? It's no good just rushing off."

Carl was still breathing angrily, still glaring at Rob. "We go after those guys, right? They might have stopped for a rest. They might head back this way. Let's do something, for God's sake! We've already missed one chance to be found. We look for them; then if we can't find them — well, we come back."

Lara muttered agreement. After a few seconds, Helen shrugged and said, "Could give it a go, I suppose." Wiki nodded uncertainly.

"Rob?" asked Shawn.

"It's no use asking him!" Carl glared again. "He's too bloody feeble to do anything."

Rob saw the same contempt he'd felt for his father being turned on him. His face went hot, and he glared back at Carl.

"All right, Macho Man! We go after them!" The words felt wrong as he spoke them, but Rob swept on. "But we all go; you never divide up your party. And we take some food and gear with us in case something goes wrong."

Lara broke in. "Let's go now! Come on, Carl! If these others want to waste time, they can catch us up."

Shawn smacked his hands together. "Rob's right. We all go. And we take some basic gear. If we find those guys, we get them to come back here too. Now hurry!"

While the others scrabbled at their gear, Rob tried to think through the next few hours. Water, warmth, wetness: the tramper's big three. He pushed waterbottle, jumper and parka into his pack. Food: he took biscuits from the piles Helen had laid out neatly under one tent fly. He hesitated, then without knowing why, added a bag of rice. First aid kit. He looked up to find Shawn watching him and following his moves.

"Always do what the experts do," grunted Shawn, and tossed a packet of instant noodles into his own pack.

Rob thought again. He slipped his Swiss Army knife into his side pocket, then hurried across the clearing and into the trees where Harvey's body lay. From inside the guide's pack, he pulled a spare shirt — a red-and-blue one, he noted with relief. Then he stopped dead.

Food! Harvey's share of the food would still be in his pack. Rob was reaching in again when Lara's voice shrilled. "What are you doing?"

"There'll be extra food in Har—" Rob began. But Lara wouldn't let him finish.

"Leave him! Leave him alone! You're sick!" Carl joined in, "Come on! We're going, even if you're not!"

Rob's mouth tightened. He grabbed the shirt and scrambled back to where the others were shrugging on quarter-full packs. "Come on!" Carl called again.

Rob hesitated. Everything his father had told him about tramping said you never went rushing off like this. Yet — and he thought angrily again of his father's sad silences at home — maybe Carl was right; maybe doing *anything* was better than just sitting. Anyway, they'd be back in a few hours.

Carl was already heading into the trees, with the three girls behind him. Shawn was looking back at Rob, who stood staring uncertainly at the tent flies and gear now lying scattered around the clearing. "OK, mate?" Shawn asked.

"Go that way!" Rob pointed to the left, where even through the thick bush they could see the ground rising. "Follow the ridge. It'll get us up faster."

Carl muttered, but turned where Rob pointed. He plunged on, jumping over logs, pushing through high ferns and supplejack. Rob knew it was wrong, starting off so fast and wild. He knew also it was no use trying to tell Carl.

By the time they reached the line of the ridge, people were panting and heaving for breath. Carl glanced behind him, then yelled furiously, "What are you doing?"

Rob was twenty metres back, half-hidden by the trees. He was hacking at Harvey's red-and-blue shirt with his knife.

"I'm leaving a trail." A strip of red came away, and he tied it quickly to a skinny branch. "We've got to find our way back, remember."

Carl snarled. "You're wasting time! You're trying to slow us down!" But Lara was gasping, "You've got to—go slower, Carl! Can't go—this fast!"

Carl turned without a word and began pushing up the slope. The others followed. At the back, Rob tore more bits off the shirt and tied them to branches. He pulled other small branches down till they split, white and gleaming. Ahead of him, he saw Shawn tearing off big fern leaves and jamming them in logs, smacking at trees with a stick so that marks and smears were left on the trunks. A trail of sorts was being made.

The slope grew steeper. Trees still blocked any view, but the undergrowth was thinner. Then the trees themselves began to get smaller. Glimpses of a sky ribbed with thin white clouds appeared. Carl pushed on, flat out. The three girls fought grimly after him. Rob and Shawn concentrated on marking the trail.

The ridge narrowed. The ground fell away on either side, dropping till trees hid everything below from sight. They went up a slope so steep that they were almost on hands and knees, then around and up a bank of tree-roots and ferns. "Need—a hand!" gasped Lara. Carl wrenched her up impatiently, and ploughed on. He took another ten or so steps. Then slowly he came to a halt. The others panted up behind him and stared.

They were out of the trees. Ahead of them the ground sloped up sharply, dotted with stunted, wind-blasted shrubs, and lichen-covered boulders as big as station-wagons.

Above this again, shingle slides angled up like grey ugly fans against the mountains. Black and barren and streaked with dirty summer snow, the great shapes of Hill 50, The Dome, Kawahine, bulked against a pale sky. A thin wind keened past, and all six of them shivered. There was no sign of human life to be seen.

Thirteen

"They *must* have come up here!" Carl's chest was still heaving. His T-shirt was dark with sweat. "We heard their shots! Where else could they go?"

Shawn climbed on to the nearest big boulder. Helen, Wiki and Lara slumped on the ground. Rob eased off his pack and placed it on the stony ground. "They'll go where the deer go," he told Carl. "And the deer go anywhere."

On top of the boulder, Shawn peered around. "Nothing. Not even a bird."

"Let me look!" Carl began scrambling up, slipping and clawing. Shawn shook his head and slid carefully back to the ground.

"Hey!" Carl bellowed when he was on top of the boulder. "Hey! Help! Hello!" His yells dwindled into the emptiness. The wind moaned again, and the dark-haired boy hugged himself against the sudden cold. Silently he climbed down.

"Save some water," Rob advised, as the others sprawled

dejectedly on the ground. "We'll need it before we get back to camp."

"I didn't bring a water bottle," Lara muttered. Without a word, Helen passed hers across.

"Jeez, it'd freeze the feathers off a brass duck up here." Wiki was pulling on her jacket as the wind blew again.

From the corner of his eye, Rob saw Carl search through his pack, then huddle in the most sheltered place he could find, trying to pull down the sleeves of his thin T-shirt. Rob looked up to where the thin white ribs of cloud had spread across more of the sky. Mares' Tails, his father called them; bad-weather clouds. He remembered Harvey's forecast of rain. Thank hell we've got the way back to camp marked, he told himself.

They ate one-and-a-half biscuits each from the packet Rob had brought. They divided up two oranges that Helen was carrying.

"Hope you enjoyed your meal, ladies and gents," Wiki tried to grin. "Sorry I forgot the champagne."

"Wish someone'd put a cork in *you*," Helen told her friend.

"Are we going higher up?" Lara asked. Her voice was flat and empty.

Nobody spoke. Carl stared at the stones between his feet.

"We haven't got the right gear," Rob said finally. The others looked relieved.

Shawn stood, shivered as the wind hit him, and turned up the collar of his blue jacket. "Let's get down into the trees where it's sheltered."

They turned their backs on the rock faces and jagged ridges of the mountains, and headed back the way they'd come.

Going down the ridge was slow and silent work.

It was slow because Shawn in front kept pausing to check for the signs he and Rob had left. Sometimes a strip of shirt could be seen ten metres away. Other times they had to stop while Shawn, and Helen who was second in line, searched left and right till they found a broken branch or a mark on a tree-trunk.

It was silent because everyone was depressed after not finding the hunters. Carl and Lara said nothing, just walked with their eyes on the ground. Even Rob, who hadn't wanted to leave the camp, felt gloomy. We'll light the fire when we get back, he decided. That'll make people feel better.

Because they were moving slowly as they looked for the trail, the day felt cooler. Jerseys and parkas stayed on. After a while, Rob looked ahead to where Carl was wearing only his thin T-shirt. He worked his parka out of his pack, caught up to the dark-haired boy, and passed the parka over. Carl looked at him, then put the yellow PVC on without a word.

When an hour had gone, Rob took Shawn's place at the front. Tramping books all said you should do this — it was a strain searching for the trail.

Mark by mark, they found their way down. They passed a tree whose split grey trunk Rob had fixed in his mind as they struggled up. His watch showed 1.57 pm; they should be back in the clearing soon after 3 o'clock for a cup of tea. Straightaway Rob felt better.

"We're doing OK," he said, over his shoulder. Then, because he wanted somehow to make up for things, "Like a turn in front, Carl?"

"All right," said the dark-haired boy, without much enthusiasm. But he came forward. Lara went behind him.

Rob dropped back to the rear with Shawn. In the middle, Helen began telling Wiki that in future she could buy her own raffle tickets. The first giggle of the day was heard.

Rob had been wanting to ask something. "Hey, Shawn? Remember when you were up that tree the other night? You said you'd done a rock-climbing course."

"Yeah, it was cool. Wouldn't want to go on those mountains back there, though."

Rob found himself hurrying to catch the other boy up. Ahead, Wiki and Helen were moving more quickly, too. Carl goes downhill almost as fast as he goes uphill, thought Rob.

To Shawn, he said, "Hey, maybe when we get home, you could teach me some of it?"

They both halted suddenly. In front, Wiki and Helen had stopped too. Carl was hesitating by a big fallen tree that sprawled under a mound of ferns and mosses. Lara was staring exhaustedly at the ground.

"See the next mark?" Rob called, suddenly anxious.

Carl wouldn't meet his eye. "Nah. Last one was back up there somewhere. We keep going down, we'll find them, won't we? If you made them good enough."

Wiki looked hard at the fallen tree, then stared around at the thick bush. "I don't recognise this part at all."

Fourteen

For a moment, it seemed that Shawn was going to hit Carl. The blocky boy took two steps forward, his fists bunched. Rob felt anger swell inside his own chest.

He spoke loudly, to himself as much as anyone. "Stop!" Then, more quietly, "Everyone just stop."

Shawn halted, breathing hard. The others were silent.

"OK." This time, Rob never thought for a second about Carl's sneers. "We don't go on down. Ridges get further apart the lower you go, so we could end up miles away from camp. We spread out, but we make sure we can see one another. We go very slowly back up, looking for signs of the trail. And one of us — Shawn? — marks where we're going now."

They formed into a rough line, Carl still not looking at anyone, Lara blank-faced and pale, Shawn chewing on a twig that he occasionally held between his fingers like a cigarette. The close growth, the dropping, root-tangled ground, and the knots of fern and supplejack meant that their line covered about thirty metres only. Rob knew that they might already be much further off the trail than that.

"Even if you think it's just a mark, call out," he told them. "And keep watching the others."

Progress back up the ridge was painfully slow. When anybody clambered up a bank or over a log, those on either side had to wait. Lara didn't seem to be looking at all; just plodding uphill.

After half-an-hour, Helen called, "There's something here!" But when the others gathered eagerly around her, they found just a mark on a tree-trunk from an old broken branch. "Sorry," muttered Helen.

Wiki patted her on the shoulder. "No worries. Tell you what — first person to find the trail gets a big hug and a sloppy kiss."

At nearly four o'clock, they stopped for another half-biscuit and a few mouthfuls of water. Their hands and knees were filthy where they'd climbed over logs. Lara had a long scratch down one leg and a tear in her shorts where she'd slipped while hauling herself up a bank. They were hungry, worn-out and frightened.

"We'll go for another hour-and-a-half," Rob said, trying to sound confident. "Then we'll decide what to do."

They stopped after just an hour. By that time, the ground had somehow turned so that they were struggling along the side of a slope. It was still hard to see more than ten steps ahead on the steep, tree-choked ground, but Rob knew this wasn't the way they'd come.

Then Helen called, "Hey, Lara!" They turned to see the other fair-haired girl sitting on the ground, head between her knees. When they reached her, she was crying hopelessly.

"We've gotta stop," Carl said. Shawn grunted agreement. Wiki said, "Let's just flop, eh? Sit and think. Putting it politely, I'd say we were deep in the crap."

They sprawled exhausted among the damp ferns of the slope for half an hour. Helen and Wiki took turns sitting with their arms around Lara, who crouched and whimpered against them.

Finally Shawn spoke. "We're gonna have to spend the night here." He pointed to where the light in the treetops was starting to take on a duller, golden tinge. "Come on. Better get organised while we've got plenty of time. Let's see what we've got."

It didn't take long. A jacket or parka each. About two bottles of water. Two packets of biscuits, an orange, the rice and noodles that Rob and Shawn had brought.

Wiki had a tent fly; as she pulled it out, something fell from the tangled nylon. "Hey, must have got caught up when I packed it!" she exclaimed, holding up the chocolate whose wrapping she had used to try and light the fire in the clearing.

"Hell!" groaned Helen. "Now she'll *never* try to be tidy!" Helen herself had a sleeping bag, which she unzipped and tucked around Lara. An aluminium mug, the first aid kit, a notebook of Rob's, some spare socks. No Primus, no matches. Rob thought of the food in Harvey's pack. And, with a lurch, of Harvey's map and compass.

"Tent over us or under us?" Shawn asked.

"Over," said Rob. "All the ferns we can find go under us."

For the next half-hour, Rob and Shawn and Helen and Wiki, with help from Carl when he wasn't slumped against a tree, wrenched and snapped the big green fronds from tree ferns, and scooped up the brown ones lying on the ground. As the light through the trees faded, they spread a springy mattress as big as a king-size bed on some flattish ground between two trees. Live trees — "Never camp under dead trees," Rob's father had told him once. "They might just choose tonight to fall on you."

"Take it in turns to sleep in the middle," Shawn said. "Warmer there."

"Promise you won't tell my boyfriend?" begged Wiki. She turned to Rob, who waited for yet another wet Wiki joke. Instead, the girl murmured, "You did really great today, Rob. I reckon your Dad would be proud of you." Then she turned away to where Helen was watching, and started ordering her friend around again.

Helen's spread-out sleeping bag covered two people. Wiki's tent-fly covered the other four. "An hour under the sleeping bag; two hours under the tent-fly?" asked Shawn. Nobody cared enough to argue.

They ate a half-biscuit and two squares of chocolate each, then huddled together in jackets or parkas under the thin coverings. "No time to be shy, boys and girls. Cuddle up tight," said Wiki. Rob knew she was right, but he didn't dare look as she sandwiched herself in between him and Shawn. The thick-set boy was murmuring to Helen, and when Rob crawled out after an hour to let Carl in under the sleeping bag, he saw that Shawn was holding the tall girl's hand. What a time to start! Rob thought.

After a while, in spite of the thin tent fly, his empty stomach and the prickly ferns beneath, Rob felt drowsiness creeping up on him. Thank God. Maybe in the morning, things would look better.

Then it began to rain.

Fifteen

SUNDAY 11 JANUARY, 1.21 pm. On the Ground.

Something trickling down his forehead. Sweat. Can't be; he hasn't drunk enough to sweat. Blood, then. Yes, it must be blood.

SUNDAY: 11 JANUARY, 1.21 pm. In The Air.

Base to Victor Delta and Victor Echo: Over.

Victor Delta to Base: Yes Dave? Over.

Victor Echo to Base: Come in Dave. Over.

Base to Victor Delta and Victor Echo: Red ground party

have just been talking to a couple of hunters who were up shooting near Hill 50 and The Dome on Thursday. They say there were no signs of anybody in that area. I think we'd better try the river valleys again. Do a Noise-Up run and see if that brings anyone into the open. Over.

Victor Delta to Base: OK Dave. Out.

Victor Echo to Base: Roger Dave. Out.

When the first drops smacked on to the tent-fly, Rob thought they were just leaves from the trees above. Then he heard Helen's groan: "Oh no, it's raining!"

The others, except for Lara, struggled half-upright. Another drop hit Rob on the back of his neck and ran under his collar. He shivered.

Wiki was urging, "Come on, people. Sit up and let's all get under the fly. Keep the sleeping bag under it too, eh? Come on. Squeeze close together and we can all fit."

Rob pressed himself into a huddle with the others, knees drawn up so he used as little room as possible. Shawn tugged Lara into a half-sitting position, flopped against Carl's shoulder. Then he, Rob and Wiki pulled and spread the fly till it was finally spread out over them.

"Don't move too much or the water'll come through," said Rob. "Hold the fly up so the water runs off on to the ground."

Back to back, legs pulled up under the fly till cramp meant they had to be stretched out into the pattering rain, feeling the shivers that ran through the whole group, too miserable to talk, they waited for day.

FRIDAY: 9 JANUARY, 3.52 am.

The morning came slowly, grey and unfriendly. The rain

pattered on, easing sometimes, then coming in harder flurries. The trees dripped heavily and steadily. Their trunks were black-streaked with damp. Rob looked at the faces around him, shadowed under parka hoods, or pale and strained, with damp hair lying heavy across their skulls, eyes half-closed and vague. If only I'd made us wait at camp, he thought. Wait and stay calm. Let things take their course.

Without warning, a wave of love and sadness for his father and dead mother surged inside him. It was so sudden and powerful that his whole body jerked, and he gasped aloud.

The others stirred and groaned. Lara crouched closer to Carl. Shawn looked around at Rob and gave him a tired nod. Wiki yawned, then shivered. "Aw hell. I thought it was just a bad dream."

They ate the last of the chocolate, and the remaining orange. They ate the biscuits, leaving just one each, and drank half the water. When Helen asked if they shouldn't save more food, Rob said, "Get as much energy as we can. It'll help us when we move."

"Move?" Carl stared. "You're the one who keeps wanting us to stay, for God's sake!"

"We've got to get water," Rob replied. "And we need better shelter than this."

"Are we going to look for the trail again?" Helen asked.

Nobody spoke. Then Shawn said, "Don't reckon it's much use. Rain's probably ruined half the signs now."

More silence. Then Wiki asked, "We going up or down?"

Rob thought of the cold wind, the boulders and mountains above the tree-line. He looked at Lara, grey-faced and slumped. "Down. That way we can find a creek. And if there's a creek, there should be some open ground where Search and Rescue can see us."

Shawn stuffed Helen's sleeping bag into his pack. "I'll carry this. I'm gonna be a real gentleman today." Carl still had Rob's parka; he said nothing about giving it back. They folded the tent fly into an oblong and tied it around Lara with its own cords, like an extra raincoat. The pretty, fair-haired girl was slack-mouthed and silent. She seemed to have sunk into herself.

The rain still pattered through the treetops as they slithered down the slope, stiffly at first, then with circulation slowly coming back to their legs. The ground grew steeper, till they had to grab at roots and clumps of ferns to slow themselves. Wiki and then Shawn held a fistful of Lara's tent-fly raincoat, telling her when to move and when to stop.

After twenty minutes, another bush-slope began appearing through the trees, angling down to meet their own one. Rob knew they must be getting close to the valley bottom.

Another five minutes, then Helen called, "I can see water." The others slid and scrambled down beside her.

They were standing on the edge of a bank, which dropped straight down for about five metres to a skinny bed of rain-wet boulders, so narrow it looked more like a ditch. A little stream threaded among the rocks, over grey-white beds of sand. Their drinking water problems were over, at least.

Their other problems weren't. The banks of the stream were so close together that even from where they stood, they had to stretch their necks to look down into the narrow bed. When Rob peered out and up, through the trees, only a sliver of grey sodden sky could be seen. There was no way a Search and Rescue helicopter could ever spot them down here.

Sixteen

A few minutes scrambling and sliding along the edge of the bank brought them to where a tree had slipped into the stream, roots and all, making a rough ladder of branches down to the water.

They arrived among the boulders, filthy, damp and aching. The stream itself was dirty with mud where it wound past the base of the fallen tree, so they cupped hands and drank from the water that dripped down the opposite moss-covered bank.

"C'mon, Lara, have a drink," Wiki encouraged. Lara said nothing, just stared at the streaming moss for a few moments, then half-filled her hands and drank clumsily.

"She's not gonna be able to keep going," Wiki muttered to the others.

"The rest of us could go on? Come back for her when we find . . . something?" Carl's voice trailed away.

"You don't leave an injured person by themselves!" Rob was surprised at the anger in his voice. "And she counts as injured."

"Shall we keep going down here for a bit?" Helen jerked her head at the stream. "See if it joins a bigger one later on?"

Shawn grunted agreement. "No use staying here. That's for sure."

For most of the next hour-and-a-half, the stream ran between dripping banks so close and steep that the six were able to balance themselves with a hand against one of the moss-and-fern-covered walls. Among the boulders, the water trickled past little curves of sand like tiny picnic spots. If they weren't so tired, hungry and scared, Rob thought, they might have found it beautiful.

And if they weren't so wet. The pattering showers had turned to silent soaking rain, which streamed down on them as they stumbled along in single file.

Soon it had soaked through Rob's jersey and T-shirt. He plodded on at the back of the party, head down, sodden boots splashing in and out of pools in the narrow bed. Inside his head, words had begun thudding over and over to the rhythm of his feet. "Safety Rule—Sit And Wait—Safety Rule—Sit And Wait." Ahead of him, the others lurched and sloshed.

Rob stopped when the figures in front stopped. At the head of the line, Shawn turned. His fair hair lay streaked across his wet, dirty face.

"How about we go over there for a bit?" Shawn pointed through the slanting rain to where the stream curved ahead. Another tree had fallen across the narrow bed, its roots weakened where water had scooped the bank from under it. Overhanging bank and overhanging trunk made a hollow like a shallow cave. The floor of damp grey sand was scattered with twigs and leaves.

The others stood wet and wretched. Carl held one of Lara's elbows. The girl was swaying on her feet.

Clear and sharp into Rob's mind came the knowledge that never again could he feel as low as he felt right now. He mumbled something and jerked his head towards the hollow.

They dropped packs and crouched beneath the overhang. As soon as they stopped moving, the cold and wet of their clothes had them shaking and shivering. Rob thought numbly of the Primus and matches back at camp.

Wiki must have been thinking the same, for she muttered, "Anyone know how to rub two sticks—two *wet* sticks—together?"

Shawn, already chewing on a small twig, suddenly exclaimed and jerked upright. He grabbed his pack and scrabbled inside a pocket under its flap.

"Now who reckons smoking is bad for your health?" he demanded, and held up a yellow cigarette lighter.

It took over an hour before the fire was finally burning.

They tore pages from Rob's notebook. With his Swiss army knife, he and Helen split twigs and sliced open small branches from the floor of the hollow, to reach the dry wood inside. Wiki and Carl broke off dead tree roots poking through the overhang.

As Shawn flicked his lighter three times before it sparked, they held their breath. When flames began licking out of the pile of twigs and wood, Wiki yelled "Yes!", then clapped a hand over her mouth as her yell blew the flames sideways.

Half the smoke stayed in the overhang, making eyes smart and water. They couldn't have cared less. Every twig and leaf in the shelter was added to the flames. Helen and Carl collected wood wedged among the stream boulders. Rob and Wiki and Shawn twisted and tore dead limbs from the fallen tree. As the fire grew bigger, even wet wood hissed and glowed. Lara began to look less miserable.

One by one, jerseys and socks were held near the flames to dry. So were T-shirts and even shorts. ("Turn your backs, you guys," ordered Wiki. "Shut up, Savage!" hissed Helen. "Jeez, you're embarrassing!")

Shawn, wearing only undies and Rob's parka, rushed out for more wood and came back grinning. While the rain fell harder outside the hollow, spitting sometimes at the edge of the fire, Helen wedged a branch through the handle of the aluminium mug and heated some water, into which they dunked the last biscuits. After that, they took turns to cook the packet of rice from Rob's pack, a mug at a time. It tasted horrible; it tasted wonderful.

Warm, half-damp and half-scorched, filthy and weary, reminded by the rice that they hadn't had any sort of meal since breakfast yesterday, they sprawled and dozed through the rest of the day.

Then, as the grey light began to darken and the rain still poured down, they collected every bit of wood they could find in the streambed or beside the fallen tree, till a pile a metre high stood beside the fire, steaming in the heat.

Even Lara helped. "Thanks, everybody," she said, as she found two grains of soggy rice left in the mug, and scooped them into her mouth with a grimy finger. "Thanks and sorry." Wiki and Helen both hugged her.

"They'll be looking for us tomorrow," Rob said, as the fire crackled in the darkness and they huddled under the tent-fly and the sleeping bag. "Might even be looking for us now."

"We gonna stay here?" Carl asked sleepily.

Rob hesitated. He thought how weird it sounded — macho man Carl asking if they were going to stay put. "I reckon we need to move on a bit. Find some place where Search and Rescue can see us. The stream must get wider further down."

Silence — part-hope, part-fear, part-exhaustion, settled on the six.

Tiredness helped Rob sleep. Worry and all the aches in his body helped bring him awake. Ten times or so during the night, he jerked up from dreams that fell apart as he woke. Once, Carl was piling more wood on the fire. Another time, Helen and Shawn were murmuring together.

Between midnight and 3.10 am by his watch, he drifted in and out of sleep, while rain fizzed at the far edge of the flames.

Twice during that time, he got up and dropped branches on the fire. As he stared into the orange-and-blue flames, he thought of Harvey lying under the tree beside the clearing. He felt glad that Wiki had said her words over him.

When Rob lay down the second time, Lara turned over in her sleep and pressed up against his back. Her breath warmed his neck. Hell, thought Rob, if only the guys at school could see me now! And what would Mum say! The last three months stabbed at him again, but with less pain than before. Then he was asleep again.

Seventeen

SUNDAY: 11 JANUARY, 2.04pm. On the Ground.

The pain in his knee isn't so bad now. If he keeps walking, it'll go. If he keeps walking, everything will go. That's right, everything has gone, anyway. There's just him now. Come on, Rob, he tells himself. Come on.

SUNDAY: 11 JANUARY, 2.04 pm. In the Air.

Victor Echo to Base: You there Dave? Over.

Base to Victor Echo: Yeah, come in Tim. Over.

Victor Echo to Base: Dave, I'm pretty sure they can't be in any of the riverbeds between Nine-Mile Creek and the Wai-Iti Saddle. We've done Noise-Up runs along them all, and nobody showed. Want us to go back towards Boulder Creek and that part we looked at yesterday? Over.

Base to Victor Echo: I think Ken wants to do that, Tim. Over.

Victor Echo to Base: Yeah, fair enough. Whatever Ken wants. OK, we'll come and refuel, and check what's happening. Over.

SATURDAY: 10 JANUARY, 5.33 am.

"Rob! Rob!" A hand was pushing at him. Rob tried to pull the bedclothes up over his head, to shut out the voice. He felt the gritty sand against his cheek, and came awake with a jolt. Shawn was kneeling beside him.

"We got a problem." Shawn nodded to where the fire showed lines of steadily slanting rain.

Even above the crackle and hiss of flames and the rustle of rain, Rob could hear the new sound. A dull, growling, grumbling sound, like a concrete mixer slowly turning.

Beyond the fire, a different colour of darkness paused and swirled for a second, then swept on. Rob felt his stomach go cold.

When he crawled to the edge of the hollow, he gasped. The skinny little stream they'd trekked down yesterday was a dark rush of water, piling and tearing around nearly-covered boulders. Small branches whirled along on its surface.

"It's coming up fast." Shawn pointed to a stick standing in the sand at the water's edge, just outside the hollow. "Put that there half-an-hour ago, and the river's got right up to it since then."

The others were awake now, staring in fright and disbelief at the sweeping water. Never make camp in a streambed, Rob heard his father say. He also heard Harvey as they crossed the Awanui Gorge: "A day's rain on Kawahine, and that river tears through here with whole trees on it." What a dork he'd been!

"We'll have to move," Rob said. He looked at his watch—5.40 am. "Look, we'll wait half-an-hour till it's light. Then we've gotta get out: find a place where we're safe from the river."

Shawn looked at the black racing water. "You reckon we can handle that."

Rob was already wrenching at the wood-pile, hauling out the two longest branches. "We'll need these: Carl and me on one, with Lara in the middle; you and Helen take the other, with Wiki in the middle. Wrap your arms around the branch and it'll help hold you against the current. We'll go till we find a safe bit on the bank, then we'll get out."

Twenty minutes later, the river was hissing at the edge of the fire. "Leave your pack waistbands undone," Rob said, as they stooped scared and shivering under the overhang. "Then you can get the pack off if you go under." He stared into the cold grey light beginning to grow outside the hollow, and the dirty water swirling past. "Come on."

As they emerged from under the bank, the rain thrashed at them. The stream which yesterday had barely covered their boots now rushed thigh-high, even waist-high, heaving and snatching at them.

But the two long branches kept them together and upright. On either side of Lara, Rob and Carl slipped, banged knees and elbows against boulders, but kept working downstream. Behind them, Wiki, Helen and Shawn followed carefully, avoiding where the other three stumbled, following where it seemed slightly easier.

The bed of the stream was invisible beneath the hurrying brown water. But Carl, who'd yelled "No!" when Rob offered to lead, probed with his foot, sank to his waist or else found shallower water, and led them on step by step. After fifteen minutes, there was nothing in the world but the rain, their gasping breath, and the churning river.

Suddenly it was lighter ahead. Proper morning, Rob thought dazedly.

No. Another thirty metres or so further on, the stream curved again. On one side, its almost vertical banks gave way to a gentle slope of feathery toi-toi, leading up into the bush. A wider triangle of dirty grey sky sagged above it.

"There!" Rob yelled. "We can get out there!"

Carl saw the escape route at the same time. He swung around in the water and lifted one arm to point. His feet slipped, and he floundered to keep balance. His end of the branch jerked from his arms, bucking and swinging in the water as Rob fought to hold on. It clubbed into Carl's side, throwing him against a boulder. The same wild swing tore the branch from Lara's grasp. She grabbed at it, missed, and vanished under the water.

Eighteen

Rob's yell was lost in the screams from behind him, as Wiki, Shawn and Helen saw Lara disappear into the tearing river. Even as he dropped his end of the branch and began ripping at his pack straps, he heard them plunging towards him.

"Help Carl!" he shouted. His pack fell from his shoulders and the river whipped it away. He took a breath and half-fell, half-threw himself into the water where Lara had gone.

With no branch to steady him, and his whole body under the surface, he was tossed around like clothes in a washing machine. Leaves, twigs and sand in the churning stream flicked and stung his face, and made him squeeze his eyes almost shut. He could hardly see, anyway; the dirty water and half-dawn darkness made sure of that.

Rob let the current sweep him along and hoped it would take him wherever Lara had gone. He stretched out his arms, groping for a touch of her. Nothing. Then a boulder jolted into his shoulder, and he floundered up, dragging and crowing for air.

Back upstream, frighteningly far back, he glimpsed Wiki and Helen holding Carl against the rocks. He saw Shawn too, fighting downstream towards him, snatching off his own pack. Rob grabbed another breath, stretched out his arms, and went under again.

Under, and straight into something that twisted and gave way, turned and bumped against him for a second, before rolling away in the current. Rob's first thought was that he'd touched a huge eel. He whipped back his arms and hunched his body in terror. Just as suddenly, he knew what it was. He lunged forward, but his hands clutched at empty water. He lunged again, touched what felt like soggy string ends, grabbed desperately, and came snorting to the surface, pulling Lara after him by her long hair.

He reeled on the rocky streambed, trying to keep his balance. He was too exhausted to do more than cup Lara's chin with his other hand and hold her face above the surface. The girl's mouth hung open, and some of her hair trailed inside it. Her eyes were closed; her body lolled limply. Her pack still hung from one shoulder, dragging her back into the swollen stream.

A weight banged into Rob's side. He lurched and almost went under. Lara's head dipped into the water again. Then Shawn was clutching him by the elbow, grabbing with another hand at Lara's shoulder and hauling her back above the surface.

"Bank!" yelled Shawn, right into Rob's ear. "Get her to the bank!"

Rob saw that the current had carried him downstream until he was almost opposite where the high banks gave way to the slope of toi-toi. Upstream, Wiki and Carl were still clinging to the rock. Helen was struggling towards the two boys and Lara.

Gasping, panting, shouting to themselves as much as to each other, Rob and Shawn part-carried, part-dragged Lara towards the river's edge.

Their feet slipped on unseen stones, and the girl's hips banged into a boulder. "Lara!" yelled Shawn. "Help us! Lara!" No sound; no movement. Lara's head stayed flopped forward.

They battled their way between two rocks and into a muddy cleft where toi-toi grew right down to the edge. Rob grabbed a fistful of long green leaves, wrenched, and dragged himself out of the water. Beside him, Shawn also struggled ashore. By one arm and by the pack still held with twisted straps to her other arm, they heaved at Lara until the top half of her body sprawled across the boulders and into the toi-toi.

They collapsed beside her, unable to move another metre. Rob could hear his breath and Shawn's, dragging in and out of their lungs. "Aaaah-aaah! Aaaah-aaaah!"

Lara's face was just in front of Rob. Rain streamed down on it, joining the river water that wound across her forehead and cheeks from her matted hair. In the cold grey of dawn, her skin was the colour of dirty pastry. She's drowned, Rob knew. She's drowned.

Nineteen

The sound of more gasping breath. Helen came stumbling up out of the rushing stream to where the other three sprawled among the rocks and toi-toi. The tall girl was drenched too, wet socks flopping down over her boots, water pouring from her sodden parka. Her eyes stared at them out of a white face.

Rob started choking something about Carl. Helen took no notice. She went down on her knees beside Lara. She grabbed one shoulder and shook the other girl hard — so hard that Lara's arm flopped up and down.

"Lara! Lara, can you hear me! Wake up, Lara!"

No movement.

"Off—rocks!" Helen blurted at the boys. "Move her!"

Rob and Shawn staggered to their feet. They seized one of Lara's arms each, pulled at her again without caring how her legs scraped over the stones, and almost threw her another metre into the toi-toi. She lay on her back, totally still.

Helen crouched beside her again, shaking and calling her. Nothing. She's drowned, Rob told himself again. It's too late. She's drowned.

Helen tilted Lara's head back, lifting her chin with the fingers of the other hand. She tilted her own head, put an ear to the other girl's mouth, and rested the palm of one hand on her chest.

"A-B-C," Rob found himself muttering. He knew what Helen was doing. A - B - C: open Airway; check Breathing; start Cardiac Compression. The first three steps of CPR resuscitation—he'd learned them too, on the Bush Safety Courses with his Dad.

Now Helen took Lara's nose between thumb and finger, and pinched it shut. She drew a deep breath, put her mouth over Lara's slackly-open lips, and blew. Lara's chest lifted, then stopped. Helen blew again. Once more the other girl's chest heaved and was still.

Helen put two fingers beside Lara's neck, where the big carotid artery lay. She waited a second, gasped "Come *on*, Lara!" and reached both hands over towards the unmoving chest.

On hands and knees, Rob scrambled forward to help. "You—do breathing!" he began to say. "I'll—" He collided with Shawn, lurching forward beside him.

"I'll help!" the chunky boy gasped. "I know CPR!"

"Me too!" Rob gasped back. They gaped at each other

for a moment, then Shawn began forcing himself to his feet again. "Wiki—Carl—" he mouthed, and pushed his way back to the swollen stream.

Rob knelt beside Lara, water dripping and running on to her from his face and arms. He placed the heel of one hand flat in the middle of her breastbone, laid his other hand on top, and pushed, straight-armed and firm. "One," he grunted. "Two—Three—"

Helen stared, drew in a shuddering breath, then bent over Lara once more, waiting while Rob pushed. This is a *girl* I'm doing this to, Rob's mind told him as his hands pressed on Lara's chest. Just as suddenly, the memory came back of the warm figure asleep, snuggling against his back in the hollow under the bank. A fierce ache stabbed him. "Fourteen—Fifteen," he counted, then yelled like Helen, "Come on, Lara! Come *on*!"

The tall girl in the sodden parka breathed twice more into the other's cold white mouth. Rob pushed again, grunting out his count. Again Helen laid her fingers against the side of Lara's neck. "I—I think—" she began. Then—"Push!"

Fifteen more pushes from Rob. Two more breaths from Helen. Rob pressing again while Helen felt for the pulse.

"Stop!" she told him. Three seconds' pause while Rob held his breath. Then "Yes!" cried Helen. "Push!" As Rob's hands went back to Lara's chest, feeling now the faint thump under his palm, Helen burst into heaving, racking tears.

More pushes. More breaths. Lara twitched. A sound came from her mouth. "Push!" urged Helen again. Lara twitched a second time, groaned, flickered her eyelids. Then, as Rob grunted "Fourteen—Fifteen," once more, she sighed. As he lifted his hands, her chest rose and fell of its own accord.

"She's breathing!" Helen gasped. "She's breathing!" She threw her arms around Rob's neck, hitting him painfully on the nose as she did so. "Hell!" she gulped. "Why do I cry when I'm happy!" The two of them wrapped their arms around Lara's sodden body, pressing themselves against her. Lara's breathing jerked, then continued.

Scraping and splashing noises behind them. Rob turned his head. Shawn, Wiki and Carl were stumbling ashore. Carl's face was screwed up in pain, but he was on his feet, helping Wiki almost as much as she was helping him.

Shawn was gripping his pack. "Caught — rocks," he told Rob between chattering teeth. "Can't see — yours." The sleeping bag, Rob thought. We've still got the sleeping bag. Wiki and Carl were staring past him at Lara. Rob could see the terror in their eyes. He started to scramble up to tell them it was all right, but Helen was already there.

"She's alive!" the tall girl blurted. Her hands went out to Wiki and Shawn. "She's alive!"

Standing there at the water's edge, the rain still pouring down on them from the ragged grey sky, the five embraced and laughed, and yelled and cried.

Twenty

"We gotta get some shelter." Wiki brought them back to reality. "We can't stay here."

She waved a tired arm at the dirty, rushing water, the

rocks, the saturated toi-toi bushes. "We're gonna get wetter and wetter."

"Up in the trees." Shawn jerked his head to where the dark bushline began, further up the slope. He looked at Carl Chadwick, now slumped against a rock and holding his side. "Can you manage?"

"I got bowled by a boulder." Carl grinned weakly at his sentence. "Yeah, I'll get there. Who'll take Lara?"

Helen's voice was firm. "We'll all take Lara."

They eased the unconscious girl's pack off her arm. The others — except for Rob's, all the packs were safe — piled theirs beside it. They grasped Lara under armpits and knees, while Carl, wincing whenever he moved, held her head.

Then they dragged, carried, pulled her through the thick and dripping toi-toi and up to the bushline. They stumbled over rocks. They gasped for stops so they could draw breath or get a better grip. Then somehow they were in among the trees, easing Lara down where a huge fallen trunk lay like a rotting wall. They collapsed beside her, not talking, not even thinking, too exhausted to care about their own misery.

After a few moments, Rob made himself move.

"Lara?" he croaked, and raised himself on hands and knees to look at her. The girl lay limp against Helen, whose arms were tightly around her. Lara's breathing was slow and shallow. Her skin was still a greyish colour, and her eyes stayed closed.

"Hypothermia," Rob said. Shawn lifted his head and stared at Lara too.

"I think she's all right," Helen said. "She's not shivering."

Rob shook his head. "If you're too cold, you can't even

shiver. You lose heat twenty times faster when you're wet. Got to get her into the sleeping bag."

"It'll be soaked," Shawn told him. "My pack went under the water."

But he and Rob tottered to their feet. "Everyone hug her," Rob said to Wiki and Carl, who crawled over to join Helen. The two boys stumbled back down through the toi-toi, to where the packs lay jumbled.

Amazingly, the sleeping bag wasn't entirely wet. Or maybe just not as wet as everything else. They unzipped it, shook it and squeezed it. They yanked off Lara's squelchy boots and pulled the bag up over her chilled body. Her arms and legs flopped as they worked her into the damp padded envelope.

Then Rob looked at Carl. "Get in."

The shivering, dark-haired boy stared at him.

"Get in," Rob repeated. "We'll take turns. It'll help keep her warm. Help keep *you* warm."

Wiki nodded. "Go on, Carl. Promise I won't tell anyone at your school. Or promise I *will* tell them, if you like."

Finally Carl was wedged in the bag with Lara. Even though she was unconscious, he tried to face the other way, till Rob told him, "Breathe on her. Go on; it all helps."

"We gotta keep moving," Shawn told the others. "Else we'll get as bad as she is."

They made their slow way down to the remaining packs. Their aching arms could manage only one quarter-full pack between two people, but they hauled them up the slope till all five lay beside the sleeping bag. There was no sign of Rob's. First-aid kit and Swiss Army knife gone, he thought. And my water bottle. He looked at the water dripping from every branch around him, and shrugged.

He and Shawn spread out the tent fly, tying it to the

dead tree and to fern clumps and fallen branches on the ground, until it made a sloping roof over the sleeping bag where Carl and Lara lay. Flurries of rain still blew in at the ends, but the drops from the trees above no longer fell thickly on them.

The other four huddled under the thin shelter. They pushed their legs inside their packs, and pulled the flaps up over their knees. Rob heard a clicking noise and saw Shawn flicking his cigarette lighter, rubbing it against his sodden pack, flicking it again. Shawn caught Rob's eye and shook his head. "No good. Flint's ruined."

No lighter. No fire. No warmth. Rob could feel the despair in the others around him.

Twenty-one

Then Helen spoke. "Arm wrestling."

As the others' jaws dropped open, the tall girl snorted. "Come on. You said we gotta keep moving. C'mon, Wiki Savage. Let's see if all your muscles are in your mouth."

Two minutes later, Rob's jaw was still hanging open as he watched Wiki, teeth gritted, slowly push down Helen's hand where they sat, elbows on their pressed-together knees. "Gotcha!" cried Wiki. Then, "C'mon, which of you guys is least chicken?"

"Me and Rob'll have a practice first," Shawn said. The two boys strained against each other. By the time Shawn's chunky arm had bent his backwards, Rob could feel the effort bringing warmth to his chilled back and shoulders.

Rob beat Helen. Shawn beat Helen (whose hand he held for rather a long time) and Wiki. Rob beat Wiki — just.

"My turn!" Carl unzipped his side of the sleeping bag and began worming out. He stopped as Lara stirred and whimpered beside him. "I think she's a bit better," he said. "Her — her front isn't so cold."

The others bent over the sleeping bag. It was true. Lara's face was losing its dead white colour. But when Rob laid a hand on her neck, it felt chill and clammy, and her breathing was still shallow and slow.

"My sleeping bag's synthetic," said Helen. "The shop reckoned it would keep warm even when it was wet."

Wiki grinned at her friend. "C'mon then, owner. You can do the next consumer test. Leave the electric blanket on and I'll go after you. Just as well it's summer, eh?"

Carl squeezed out of the bag. He gasped as the movement caught his sore side. Rob stretched out a hand and helped him up.

"Thanks," muttered the dark-haired boy. Then, in a low voice, "Look — sorry I didn't listen to you before, eh? We should have stayed put." Rob glanced away, embarrassed.

Helen meanwhile folded her long legs and began working her way into the bag to take Carl's place. She was halfway in when she stopped and pointed. "Look!"

The sky above the slope of toi-toi was no longer a cram of dark grey clouds. A bright white patch appeared, glared for a moment, then vanished. The rain thinned, fell hard, thinned again. Another, wider patch of white cloud appeared.

"They'll be searching now," Shawn said.

"Yeah," Rob agreed. "Yeah, they will."

Quarter of an hour later, Helen lay with her arms around

Lara, murmuring to her. The unconscious girl hadn't stirred again, though once her eyelids quivered.

The others, arm-wrestling forgotten, sat close together in silence, watching the sky. The rain still fell, but nowhere near as hard as before. The white, bright patches of cloud grew bigger and more frequent. Dad'll be worried sick by now, Rob thought. Or maybe he thinks we'll have done the sensible thing and stayed put.

He glanced at his watch. 9.14 am. It must have stopped under the water; must be later than that. But as he looked, the 14 flicked to 15. Breakfast time, a voice inside his head told him stupidly.

"We got anything left to eat?" Carl asked, as if he'd been reading Rob's mind.

"A packet of noodles," Rob told him. "And nothing to cook them with."

"Could soak them in water." Helen's voice came from the sleeping bag. "Be better than nothing."

Another thought tugged at Rob. "We should lay out a signal. Down there by the river. Use our packs, or make a V or an X with stones and branches and things."

Shawn grunted. "Yeah. But wait till the rain eases off a bit, eh? No use gettin' wet again now we're startin' to get dry."

More silence. Then Wiki spoke. "When I get home, I'm gonna have six blocks of chocolate."

Shawn grunted again. "I was gonna have six packets of smokes. But I reckon I must be going off them."

"Rain's nearly stopped," said Carl.

The others peered out under the edge of the tent fly. Carl was right. Only a thin drizzle was drifting down. From the branches somewhere above, a bird began to sing, fragile and bright. Further away, Rob heard a wind starting to stir and knock in the treetops.

"We'll take the packs down," he began to say. "Lay them out, so -"

With startling speed, the wind above him roared louder and louder. Not a wind — a landslide! No, a tree falling! The truth of the sound struck them all at the same time. Frantically, they began scrambling out from under the tent fly. Even Helen was thrashing inside the sleeping bag, trying to get out.

Too late. The helicopter, rotors clattering, emerged from the thinning clouds above the empty slope of toi-toi. It hovered for a moment, turning slowly. Then, a second before Shawn and Wiki stumbled out of the trees, waving their arms and screaming, it lifted up into the clouds again and flew away.

Twenty-two

For five minutes, they were too confused and excited to believe the helicopter had gone. Anyway, it must be coming back any moment. It must be!

Carl, hurrying into the open with one hand pressed to his side, yelled and waved his other arm at the clouds where the helicopter had vanished.

Wiki and Helen were talking, turning, staring in every direction. "See it? Reckon they saw us? It *was* Search and Rescue, wasn't it? They must know we're round here!"

After their first yells, Shawn and Rob were silent. Shawn didn't meet Rob's eyes. After another few minutes he muttered, "Better lay out a signal, eh? Get some branches and things."

"Yeah," Rob said. He and Shawn began to pick their way down the slope towards the river, in the rain that was falling again. The other three began to follow, but Rob stopped them.

"You guys better look after Lara, eh? Chopper'll see me and Shawn if — when it comes back. Keep listening for it. No use us all getting wet again."

Carl and Wiki seemed set to argue, but Helen, after a look at the two boys, said, "Come on, Wiki," and started moving back among the trees. Carl stayed by the bushline, staring up at the wet sky as if he expected a rope ladder to drop down at any moment.

Neither Rob nor Shawn spoke till they were nearly down by the rushing brown stream. Then Shawn pushed his matted hair off his forehead. "It won't be back, will it?"

Rob hesitated. "Could be. You can't tell."

The other boy sighed. "C'mon, Rob. I heard what you were saying about Search and Rescue stuff. That chopper's following a plan, isn't it? They'll keep moving on till they've covered every place we might be. They won't come back here for ages."

This time Rob wouldn't look at Shawn. "Yeah, I — I think that's how they do it."

Again Shawn pushed at his hair. "It's my fault. We should have started making that sign as soon as you thought of it. I put off starting the fire back where Harvey is, too. I stuffed it up, as usual."

"Crap, boy! You've been great! Look — " Rob stopped pulling at a dead branch tangled in the toi-toi. "Look — if they don't find us the first time, they'll look again. The chopper'll be back, sooner or later."

"Yeah, but what's gonna happen to us in the meantime, eh? Lara needs to be in hospital — and fast. Carl's hurt, too. We've got nothing to eat, no dry clothes, nothing to start a fire. Rob, if someone doesn't get to us in the next couple of days, we could be dead meat!"

For the next half-hour, the two boys hardly spoke. Together they wrenched and twisted bits of wood and branches from between boulders and toi-toi. They trampled around near the edge of the stream, kicking and flattening clumps of rough grass till they'd cleared an area twice the size of a garage. They laid the wood out in the shape of a big V — Require Assistance — and an X — Require Medic. Between the two letters they laid more branches and stones in the shape of an arrow, pointing towards the trees where Lara lay.

Rob looked up once towards the edge of the bush, but there was no sign of the others. Carl had given up watching the sky, and vanished.

The work warmed them a little, but they were still shivering when they finished. As he straightened up from putting a last rock in place at the head of the arrow, Shawn staggered, and grabbed at a toi-toi beside him.

"Must be gettin' weak in my old age."

Rob thought of how little they'd had to eat since they rushed from the campsite where Harvey's body lay. They were going to get weaker still.

The rain had almost stopped again. There was no sign of the sun, but glaring white patches were breaking up the wet greyness of the sky.

As Rob and Shawn made their slow way up the slope towards the trees, every toi-toi bush was glittering with raindrops. Against the green-black wall of bush, the plumes stood like giant feathers of white and gold. Dad would love this place, Rob thought.

Under the tent fly, Wiki was now in the sleeping bag with Lara. "Sorry, guys, no vacancy," she cracked, then her face went heavy again. "She's not waking up. She's still so cold."

Helen, sitting back-to-back with Carl, feet tucked inside her pack, muttered, "She needs hot food."

"Hot food!" Carl half-turned, then gasped as his sore side stopped him. "Don't be pathetic! Might as well expect a shower and TV to arrive!"

He stared up at the other boys, from eyes which now had huge, bruised-looking patches under them. "What are we gonna do?"

Rob knew what he had to say. He knew also that it broke every tramping rule in every book.

"Some of us are gonna stay here. But someone's gotta go for help."

Twenty-three

"Just two people," Rob was saying ten minutes later. "Small party travels faster."

"I'll go," Wiki said.

"I'll go with you," Helen said immediately. "You get lost in a school corridor."

Shawn spoke. "I reckon Helen and Wiki should both stay with Lara. Helen knows first aid. You're both good with her. I'll go."

"And me," Carl said, then winced again.

Rob shook his head. "Shawn and me. We'll go as soon as we're ready. No point hanging about. It's still only," he took another look at his watch, "only 10.35."

"Where'll you go?" Carl wanted to know. "We're lost. You'll just get more lost."

Two days before, Rob might have snapped back about who had got them lost. But all the sneering had gone from Carl's voice now.

"We'll keep following the river," Shawn said. "It's gotta come out of the National Park sometime. If Search and Rescue find you first, tell them that's what we're doing."

Helen looked at Rob. "You want my pack, Rob? Yours must be about 10 k's downstream by now."

"Yeah, thanks. You guys keep the tent fly. And try to keep Lara warm."

"If it gets fine we'll move her out into the sun," Wiki said. "We'll be OK. Hey, you guys take those yukky noodles. I'll hunt down a few wild chocolate bars while you're gone."

It took only five minutes for Rob and Shawn to be ready. There was hardly anything to put in their packs — the noodles and Wiki's waterbottle in Rob's; Shawn's waterbottle and a spare pair of socks in his. Before they stood up to go, Rob took off his boots and then his socks, which he and Wiki twisted and squeezed as hard as they could.

"Wet socks give you blisters," he explained to Shawn, who was doing the same to his socks with Helen.

Shawn looked up briefly from under his mat of dirty wet hair. "Don't think I'd notice if I had a blister on every bloody toe."

When the two of them were ready, they stood for a moment by the edge of the tent fly. After another short hard shower a few minutes earlier, the rain had stopped again.

"Look—" Rob began. "Mightn't be till tomorrow or the next day that we get out. So don't worry if nobody comes for a while, eh?"

None of those staying behind said anything. "Say hi to Lara for us," Shawn added, looking down at the white, still figure in the sleeping bag. "Tell her she snores."

Still none of the others spoke. Then Wiki unzipped herself from the sleeping bag and slowly stood up, pushing at her cold stiff knees.

"It was wrong to leave Harvey," she said. "You shouldn't ever leave somebody all by themselves like that, whether they're alive or dead. But it's right for you guys to go now."

She put her hands gently around the back of Shawn's neck, and held her cheek against his. Then she did the same to Rob. Her face felt cold but soft.

"Wiki's got less brains than our budgie." Helen gave Rob's hand a squeeze, and Shawn's hand a longer squeeze. "But she's right this time. She was right before, too—your Dad would be proud of you, Rob." Then, in words which brought a different face before Rob's eyes, the tall girl added, "You guys take it easy, eh?"

When he and Shawn were halfway down the slope of toi-toi, Rob looked back at the trees. Carl stood there, one hand holding his side.

He raised his other hand in a thumbs-up sign, and called, "Later, guys! We'll be right!"

When Rob looked back again, just twenty metres down the river, the other side of the slope was between him and the bushline. Carl could no longer be seen.

Twenty-four

"You go in front for thirty minutes," Rob told Shawn. "Then we'll have five minutes rest and change over. Dad and I do that sometimes when we're tramping. Seems to make things go faster."

Shawn grunted. He passed Rob a long skinny branch he'd pulled from between the bank and a boulder. He stooped to wrench out another jammed branch for himself. "Might need one of these again."

Using the sticks partly for balance, partly to test the depth of the brown water, the two boys edged down river. They kept as close as possible to the bank, where the water was shallower and slower-moving. It was a slow scramble, bumping ankles and knuckles on boulders, sliding down awkwardly to wade across pools. Rob knew they weren't moving much faster than someone crawling on hands and knees.

Every few minutes, Shawn paused to catch his breath. Each time, Rob gazed around at the jagged, tree-crammed ridges and slopes pressing down to the very edge of the stream. It could take us a week to get anywhere, he thought. Especially with no food; we're going to get even slower.

Half an hour had almost passed. Rob was opening his mouth to call for their first five-minute rest. Then Shawn, climbing around a log five metres in front, stopped. He looked ahead at something Rob couldn't see. He turned and gave Rob a thumbs-up sign.

They're here! Rob thought. They've found us! Banging his elbow against a boulder, half-falling to his knees in the water, he splashed to where Shawn was standing.

At first he felt anger and disappointment, as if Shawn had played some stupid trick on him. Nobody was there. Just the bed of the river, opening out to over twice its present width, with stretches of shingle and scrawny, driftwood-scattered grass, around which the water wound.

"Should be able to move a lot quicker now," Shawn was saying.

Rob breathed hard, kept quiet, and knew that Shawn was right. Now they could walk instead of scramble. If the going stayed like this, they might be out into farmland in a couple of days after all.

"I'll go in front for a while," he told Shawn, forgetting all about the five-minute break.

He climbed around the log, over more rocks, and on to a level patch of shingle, where for the first time they could walk easily and upright. As Shawn followed him out of the water, a sudden brightness spread across the valley.

Rob jerked his head up and squinted at the sky. Behind a thin veil of whitey-grey cloud, the disc of the sun appeared. Rob felt brief warmth on his face.

The sun vanished, and another line of drizzle drifted down. Then another welling of brightness, and once again the disc warmed his face and front for a few seconds before it vanished.

Now it was Rob who turned to Shawn and gave him a thumbs-up.

They stopped for lunch at 12.45 by Rob's watch. They'd been walking for two hours, and the ridges tumbling and twisting down to the riverbed around them were different from the ones where they'd started. Was it just Rob's imagination, or were they a bit lower? He said nothing to Shawn.

"Lunch" was hardly the word. Half the packet of instant noodles, soaked in a pool of browny water for ten minutes and then swallowed. They tasted too foul even to joke about.

But the sun came out, from a tiny patch of blue sky this time, and a fantail began somersaulting around the two boys as they sat, filthy elbows on filthy knees, slurping cold, slimy noodles from their hands.

"You like fantails?" Rob asked Shawn. His father always talked to him when he got tired while tramping. Rob knew it helped keep your mind on other things.

Shawn lifted sunken eyes. "Love them. Especially on toast with tomato sauce."

They exchanged feeble grins. "Come on," Rob said. "See if we can find some wild chocolate bars for Wiki."

They straightened shaky legs, shrugged raw shoulders into packs, and moved on. Behind them, the fantail fluttered, warm and plump and unworried. Then it swooped back to its nest of moss and soft bark, on a tree branch high above the water.

Twenty-five

Through the long summer afternoon, the two boys trudged across the riverbed's grating shingle. At first they rested and changed over every thirty minutes. Each time, they arranged wood from the riverbed into the shape of an arrow, pointing downstream.

The rain had stopped, though grey cloud still covered the ridgetops on either side. Sunlight came in brief gleams, and Rob could see dryish patches starting to appear on the sleeves of his parka. But he no longer lifted his face to feel the warmth. His eyes stayed down, watching his scuffed boots swinging or stumbling over the stones. His mouth was open, slack with tiredness.

The riverbed remained wide, and mostly they were able to walk normally across the stones and shingle, beside the water. Only a couple of times did they have to slip and scramble over boulders, and splash through the knee-high flow. The branches they'd been carrying lay back where they'd stopped for lunch.

But though the weather and walking surface got better, their progress got slower.

Instead of stopping every thirty minutes, they were now stopping every fifteen minutes. Each time Rob collapsed on to the shingle or a log, he could feel his legs trembling with weakness. Each time they started off again, he had to get on to hands and knees before he could stand.

When he was leading, and looked around to check on Shawn, the other boy was plodding behind him, head down, half-asleep on his feet. If Rob spoke, he got only silence or a faint grunt in return.

When Shawn was leading, Rob trudged behind, counting his steps. Every hundred paces he glanced at his watch, then started counting again. He'd given up looking at the ridges and trying to decide if they were getting lower. It hurt his neck too much to turn his head.

He was dully counting 57...58...59 to himself when he thudded into something right in front of him. He stumbled, his hands jerked, and he found himself grasping the back of Shawn's pack.

A dead tree lay sprawled across the shingle in front of them, in a tangle of branches, lichen and driftwood. Shawn was standing still against it, head bowed, not moving. As Rob came around beside him, he saw the boy's eyes were blank, and his cheek muscles were twitching.

Rob took him by the elbow. "Come on, Shawn. We'll have a proper rest. Come on, sit down."

The other boy didn't seem to hear. He kept standing, face almost touching the bleached white branch in front of him. Rob shook his arm. "Come on, Shawn. We'll stop here. I'm stuffed, too. Come on."

Shawn sank on to his knees, then sprawled sideways on the rough stones. His eyes were shut now, and his whole body lay limp.

Rob slumped beside him, back against the fallen tree, forehead on his pulled-up knees. His eyes were blurry. His body felt shaky and sick, but he knew he had almost nothing in his stomach to throw up.

When was the last time they'd had anything like a proper meal? Must have been the muesli for breakfast when they were in the clearing, the morning after Harvey died. Two — no, three — no, two days ago. And even that was pretty small. No wonder he and Shawn had hardly any strength left.

Sorry, Dad, Rob found himself saying inside his head, as the sounds of the river seemed to drift further away. Sorry, Mum. I've messed this up totally.

His eyes closed, and he lay still beside Shawn. Two valleys away, the helicopter clattered up a creekbed, climbing towards the heights of Hill 50 and The Dome. The two boys slept on.

Twenty-six

The light woke Rob. Warm light on his face. And on his body and legs. He could feel the comfort of it through his parka.

He had shifted, and was lying on his side on the shingle like Shawn. He tried to turn on to his back, and groaned out loud as every muscle and joint in his body stabbed at him.

He blinked his eyes open. Above the ridgetops, the sun shone from a blue sky flecked with a few soft clouds. The bush stood green and gentle. The river was quieter. Birdcalls chimed across the valley.

Rob focused bleary eyes on his watch. 6.54.! He'd slept right through the rest of the afternoon and the night!

Then, as his mind began working, he looked at the ridges again. No, the sun was still shining on to the far side of the valley. It was evening. Daylight Saving, so the sun was still high in the sky. But he'd slept for nearly two hours.

Another groan, from beside him. Shawn, eyes shut, jerked one arm, smacked his knuckles against a boulder, and said several interesting words.

"Social Welfare send you on a course to learn *that*, too?" Rob's voice was dry and cracked.

Shawn squinted and yawned. "Helen?" he asked groggily. Then he looked embarrassed, pushed back his floppy fair hair, and stared at the dead tree beside which they both lay. "How'd we get here?"

"You walked into it. Almost into it, anyway. Then you just stopped and stood there."

"Yeah? Must have been waiting for the traffic lights to change." Shawn licked his lips. "I'm thirsty."

Rob realised he was, too. His own lips felt thick and flaky. When he tried to swallow, his throat was sore. "Come on," he said. "We're getting dehydrated and we never noticed it."

The two of them moved painfully on to hands and knees, then used the dead tree to pull themselves upright. When Rob stood, tiny lights crawled in front of his eyes. His head felt fuzzy and floating. Shawn took a step and almost fell against the tree. "Hell," he muttered "I feel about a hundred years old."

Slowly, swaying and bumping into one another, they made their way across the shingle to where the river now flowed gentle and almost clear in its bed. It goes down even faster than it comes up, Rob thought. Wonder if we'll find my pack somewhere.

They knelt clumsily beside the water and slurped from dirty cupped hands. I suppose we should try to clean ourselves up a bit, Rob told himself. But he knew he didn't have the strength.

They drank again, then sat, looking around them. The hills *were* lower, Rob felt sure. The sun, edging down towards the ridgetops, stroked the valley with light that was golden where it touched the shingle riverbed, and almost purple among the trees. It was hard to believe that anything could go wrong in a place so lovely.

Into Rob's memory slipped the picture of his mother and father and him beside a river like this when he was little, all of them skipping stones across the water, and laughing as Rob's stones skipped once and sank. He held the memory, let it comfort him.

"Weird," said Shawn. "I'm not really hungry."

"Our stomachs are shrinking," Rob told him. "Dad says that's what starts to happen if you go two or three days without food."

Shawn grunted. "Hope they shrink some more. Then we might be able to float outa here like balloons."

After a while, they struggled back to the dead tree where their packs were. "I'm beat," Shawn muttered. His eyes were more sunken than ever, and his face was a dirty white. "Don't reckon I can go much more today."

"We won't go any further." Rob knew what his father would do if he were here. "We'll rest here for the night. Soon as it's light, we'll eat the rest of the noodles and get going again."

Having a plan made him feel better. Shawn seemed to perk up, too. From the nearest edge of the bush, they wrenched some floppy ponga fronds and a few toi-toi plumes, stopping every few seconds as their shaky arms lost strength. They sat with backs against the dead tree, close together, Rob's parka over their legs, Shawn's blue jacket around their shoulders. Half the fronds and plumes were under them; half were spread across them.

As they sat, they watched the line of shadow slide down the valley wall and across the riverbed towards them. They saw the first stars prick into sight. They waited for the short summer night to come and go.

We've got tomorrow, Rob was telling himself perfectly calmly. After that, I reckon we'll be too weak to go on. After that, it'll be too late for us and the others.

Twenty-seven

To Rob's surprise, he slept for a while. Dozed, anyway. Because suddenly it was proper night, and the sky was jewelled with brilliant stars. Shawn's head had slumped against his shoulder, and the other boy was breathing slowly and quietly.

Hope Wiki and Carl and Helen and Lara are all right, Rob thought. Hope they managed to get Lara out into the sun this afternoon. Hope Harvey's family don't take it too hard when they find out. Hope . . .

But whatever he was going to hope next had started to go fuzzy and far off, just like the stars were doing.

The second time Rob woke, it was because of the cold. Cold across his thighs. Shawn was shifting uncomfortably beside him.

"You awake?" Rob asked.

"Yeah. Are you?" Before Rob could answer, the other boy snorted. "Jeez, what a dork of a thing to ask! My legs are cold."

They moved Shawn's jacket from their shoulders to across their knees, and felt better. The dead tree at their backs still seemed to hold some warmth from the afternoon sun. Fully awake now, Rob sat and looked across the shingle that gleamed softly in the starlight. He could see the flicker of the river, and hear its chuckling noise as it slid past.

"How're you feeling?" he asked Shawn.

The figure beside him yawned. "Bit better. How about you?"

"Yeah," Rob agreed. His body still ached in every joint. He still felt weak and shaky. But the fuzzy, floating feeling in his head was gone. He looked at his watch. 1.43 am. Wonder if Dad's awake? Wonder if he's out with the search parties?

"What are you thinkin' about?" Shawn asked.

Rob was silent for a moment. Then — "My father'll be worrying about me."

Shawn was silent too. When he spoke again, his voice sounded different. "Keep thinking about him, eh? It'll help you keep going. I started thinking about my Mum this afternoon. If we — when we get out of here, I'm gonna see if Social Welfare can put me in touch with her. Maybe she's just been scared or embarrassed or something about seeing me. Worth trying, don't ya reckon?" Rob felt tears gather in his eyes. "Good one, Shawn," he managed to say.

The two of them sat quietly once more. Rob thought of his bedroom at home on a Sunday afternoon, sunlight slanting across his bed, photos of himself and his Dad from one of their tramps, pinned to the wall. He saw his Dad bring him a cup of coffee and a biscuit, and try to smile. "Quite a good film on TV if you want to come and watch," he heard him say.

If I could just be back home with Dad and my room, then I'd never leave such a safe place again, Rob told himself.

And straightaway he realised that this was what his father had been doing in the last three months. His father had been lost and frightened too. Lost and frightened and alone, and not able to tell Rob because he was trying to look after him. And so his father had stayed still, clinging to the things that made him feel safe.

I never understood till now, Dad, Rob said inside his head. When I see you again, I'll behave better. I promise.

Beside him, Shawn spoke again. His voice was slurred. "Like—to meet your Dad. He sounds—a good dude."

"He is," Rob replied. "He's really good. And you come and stay with us any time you like."

But Shawn was breathing quietly and slowly once again. Rob sat and stared up to where the black edge of the ridgeline angled down across the sky. Then he slept again, too.

Twenty-eight

SUNDAY: 11 JANUARY, 3.50 pm. On the Ground.

There's something strange ahead. The ground is different. But he can hardly see now. And he's bleeding again.

SUNDAY: 11 JANUARY, 3.50 pm. In the Air.

Victor Delta to Base: Dave! Come in Dave! Over.

Base to Victor Delta: Go ahead Phil. What's happened? What is it? Over.

Victor Delta to Base: There's something in the river below. Ken thinks—he thinks it's some of the kids' gear.

Base to Victor Delta: Tell us the moment you've checked. Victor Echo will be in your area as soon as they've finished with Harvey. Look—keep an eye on Ken, will you? Out.

SUNDAY: 11 JANUARY, 4.50 am.

They started off before it was day. Stars still stood in a sky that was starting to turn green and pink along one edge. The valley was silent, except for the river burbling among its stones.

Cold had woken them once more. 3.47 am, Rob's watch said. He and Shawn had shivered and stretched, and tried to get comfortable again, but it was no use. "It's always coldest just before dawn," Rob muttered, as he hugged his arms across his chest.

Finally they got up, wincing as aching muscles dragged at them again. They stumbled across and drank more water. They made a tiny pool with a few rocks, soaked the last half-packet of noodles in it, then pushed the slimy mass into their mouths.

"Jeez!" Shawn shuddered, as he swallowed the final mouthful. "I'm never gonna eat a bloody noodle again, even if they pay me a million bucks."

Rob said nothing. He thought of the other four somewhere behind them. He tried to imagine how they were feeling as another day began. He wondered how sick Lara was, and if Carl's side was any worse. He pulled Helen's pack on to his protesting shoulders, and began to lead the way down-river.

The first twenty minutes were the worst. They stumbled over stones in the half-light, jolting ankles and knees. They shivered in the cold. Their bodies ached from the night's hard ground. It felt as if they hadn't rested at all.

Then the few mouthfuls of noodles and the movement seemed to have some effect. They began to feel warmer. Their legs moved more easily. Suddenly the stars were gone, and the sky above the valley was a pale and glowing blue. The topmost peak of a far ridge turned gold. A pair of birds skimmed piping across the shingle in front of them. They plodded on.

It was 6.15 am by Rob's watch when they stopped for their third five-minute rest. Hell, I wouldn't even be *awake* by now at home, he thought, as they drank from the river's edge and felt the cold water spread into their cramped stomachs.

Shawn led. Rob was walking head-down, and counting his steps again as the brief energy from the food started to leave him. He was aware that the noise from the river was deeper and louder somehow, but he didn't look. When Shawn stopped, he almost walked straight into him, just as he had the afternoon before.

Fifty metres ahead of them, the shingle riverbed suddenly narrowed again, to a gorge no wider than the river itself. Another, bigger river, snaking out of a side valley to the right, joined it just before the gorge, and the water became deep and powerful once more. Rob could hear it growling and grumbling; could see it piling up and collapsing in foam as it charged between big black boulders.

From either side of the valley, steep ridges arrowed down to the very edge of the new, combined river, ending in vertical drops studded with ferns and roots and protruding rocks.

It was just like the riverbed the six of them had stumbled down two days before. But this time the river was deeper, faster, crammed with two-metre-high boulders they'd have to haul themselves over, and the banks blocking their way around were cliffs twenty metres high.

Rob stood, and looked, and felt every hope drain away.

Twenty-nine

"What are we—?" Rob began, as he lurched forward to stand beside the chunky figure in front of him.

He stopped when he saw the expression on his companion's face. Shawn stood with his head pushed slightly forward. His eyes were searching the cliff on their side of the river, measuring, planning.

"There." Shawn pointed to where a clump of runty bushes clung to the cliff-face, halfway up. "We can get up to there—those ferns below look pretty strong. Then there's those tree-roots above the bushes. They'll help."

Rob saw Shawn moving steadily and expertly up through the tree towards the dead branch of firewood on their second night, talking about his climbing course while Harvey called approval from below. But that was four days ago. Four days without a proper meal. Even walking exhausted them now.

"We can't climb that," he muttered.

Shawn shrugged. "No other way."

He was right. They couldn't possibly follow the river that smacked and thumped from boulder to boulder down the gorge. It was either climb the cliff, or sit down on the riverbed stones and wait for searchers who might not come that way again for days.

Rob thought once more of Lara and the others. He

remembered Shawn's words in the moments of despair after the helicopter had appeared and gone: if we don't get help in a couple of days, we'll be dead meat.

"Lots of footholds," Shawn was saying as they began walking again. "We should be OK. We'll take it easy."

The sunlight had crept a quarter of the way down the bush on the far side of the valley. Tiny insects danced in the air as Rob sat on a boulder and tried not to think about what was to come. A few metres away, Shawn stood staring at the cliff in front of them. He'd been standing there for five minutes.

"Right." The thick-set boy pushed his matted hair back and turned to Rob. "Come and look. Here's how we'll do it."

When Rob was beside him, Shawn began pointing. "Start with that big clump of ferns there. Up and left a bit — there's a hold where a rock fell out. Then those next ferns. Then the bushes. We'll rest there for a minute. Then up to the right with a hold on that rock. Then the tree roots. And that other bush just before the top. Looks like it's quite flat once we get up there."

Rob looked. He opened his mouth, but no words came.

Shawn gave him a lopsided grin. "No worries, mate. After all, there's these guys in America who climb the outsides of skyscrapers for fun."

If this was a skyscraper, Rob thought, I'd go inside, find a phone, and order ten takeaway pizzas.

Shawn was still talking. "I'll go first. You do exactly what I do. Call out if there's a problem. Remember — don't look down, and don't move till you know exactly where you're aiming for."

Shawn was flexing his fingers, waggling them backwards

and forwards. Rob began doing the same, and was horrified to find how much his hands were shaking.

"Don't worry," Shawn told him. "It'll stop as soon as you're climbing."

Then he walked in a slow circle across the packed sand and small pebbles at the base of the cliff, kicking at larger stones so they rolled away. "Nice soft landing if we fall. But we're not gonna fall, are we?"

Rob tried to shake his head. He found it was already shaking by itself.

"OK, then." Shawn moved to the base of the cliff. He raised one leg, kicking at the clay till there was a hole the size of a clenched fist. He pushed in the toe of one boot, stretched upwards and grabbed the clump of ferns that grew from a crevice. He straightened his leg and began pushing himself up.

"Use your legs as much as you can," he said over his shoulder to Rob.

Rob in turn moved forward to the base of the cliff. He lifted his foot and pushed it into the hole Shawn had made. He tried to swallow, found he couldn't, and started reaching for the first handhold.

Thirty

It wasn't quite as bad as Rob had thought it would be. Not quite.

He was taller than Shawn. So the handholds and footholds for which the other boy stretched were holds he could reach fairly easily. But the effort of using arms and legs to work himself upwards made him tremble with weakness. And even though he tried not to, he couldn't help glimpsing the ground getting further and further below.

Above him, Shawn climbed slowly, smoothly, checking each foothold and handhold before putting his weight on it. He *did* look down — so he could check on Rob and talk him through the next move.

From the ferns to the hole where a rock had once been. Shawn worked at the hole with his hand, widening it, making a better grip for Rob. "Close your eyes," he warned first, and Rob screwed up his face as dirt from the hole trickled and bounced off his nose and forehead.

From the hole up to another, bigger clump of ferns. Across to a third clump, with an extra hold on a rock sticking from the clay face just above them. Then Shawn was saying "Good. Plenty of room here." In the corner of Rob's eye appeared a blurred mass of green and grey. Then he was clinging with both hands to the bushes that clumped in a wiry tangle on a small ledge.

Shawn gripped a handful of Rob's jersey and pack strap, supporting him as he struggled further into the half-safety of the bushes.

"Good stuff, mate. Now listen — just close your eyes and take twenty deep breaths while I count. Then we'll get going again. We're over halfway there."

Halfway there means a drop as high as a three-storey house below me, Rob realised. If I close my eyes, I mightn't ever dare open them again.

But the deep breathing helped. "Yeah, learned that on the climbing course too," Shawn said in reply to Rob's croaking question. By the time his friend had counted

"18...19...20", Rob's legs had stopped shaking. His heart had slowed from three times its normal speed to just twice-normal.

"OK, it's the rock up there to the right. Then the tree roots. Then we've got holds all over the place to the top. You've done really well, Rob."

Once more Shawn led off. Another hole kicked into the clay face. A reach up to the rock. The other hand moving past, and grasping the first of the thumb-thick black tree-roots that straggled out of the cliff.

Rob did the same. Foot in the hole. Right hand reaching for the rock and finding it. Left hand sliding towards the tree-root. And then he froze.

Shawn, two holds further up, was watching him. "Couple of inches further," he said. "Root's just ahead of you."

Rob heard, but he stayed frozen. His left hand was flat against the cliff face. His whole body had locked still, his muscles rigid, his arms and legs refusing to move even as his mind screamed orders to them.

"I—I can't move." His voice was a terrified whisper. "I can't move."

Shawn above him spoke calmly. "It's OK. It happens. Just keep looking at the cliff, and take five more deep breaths. One . . . two . . ."

Then Rob's legs began to shake again. Uncontrollable shudders that would send him toppling from the cliff any second. "Shawn—I'm gonna fall!"

Now Shawn's voice was urgent. "Face the cliff! Just face the cliff! I'm coming down." A slithering sound, then something touched Rob's paralysed left hand. "That's my boot. Just rest your hand on it, and when I pull my foot up, let your hand come too. I'll guide it to the tree-root."

But Rob's mind was crashing into total panic. He grabbed at Shawn's boot. Grabbed and held it as sudden strength rushed back into him.
There was a gasp, a scrabble of fingers, a yell of "Rob!". Then a figure was sliding and falling down the cliff past Rob, grabbing desperately for holds. Shawn crashed into the clump of bushes. They checked him for a moment, then gave way. As Rob burrowed his terrified face against the clay, he heard another scrabbling as Shawn grabbed at the ferns further down. Then the sickening thud of a body hitting the hard sand. Then silence.

Thirty-one

Rob yelled twice. A yell that became a scream. "Shawn! *Shawn!*"
Then he was moving. Slithering and scrambling back down, all fear of falling lost in the greater fear of what he would see at the base of the cliff. He tore his palms on shrub branches, banged his knees on the rocks. He half-fell, half-slid the last two metres to the sand, gasping and moaning aloud. He turned, saw Shawn's legs twitch, and gave a great sob of relief.
The fair-haired boy lay sprawled, head on one side. Rob dropped on his knees, began to shake his friend by the shoulder, then stopped as his father's Bush Safety lessons took over.
The pulse in the big artery on Shawn's neck was steady. There was no bleeding from nose or ears. When Rob pushed down Shawn's socks and pinched each ankle hard,

the boy's legs twitched again, and he whimpered faintly. Rob began to hope.

But Shawn's right arm was twisted and buckled beneath him, and when Rob shouted his name, another whimper was the only reply.

Rob sat back on his heels. He covered his face with his hands for a few moments. He stood up, looking with vague surprise at his torn palms. He gazed around the valley and his face grew calm.

Then he took off his pack — Helen's pack — and slipped it as gently as he could under Shawn's head. He spread his parka over his friend's legs. He turned back to the cliff, and he began once more to climb.

He wasn't afraid of the climb this time. He didn't feel afraid of anything any longer. He knew what he had to do — find help for Shawn and Lara and the others. There was nothing else now but that. A corner of his mind remembered promises about himself and his Dad. They could wait.

He was up at the bushes with their splintered branches before he knew it. He went on, from the rock to the root that had stopped him in terror just fifteen minutes ago. Then more tree roots. A clump of ferns. Another bush. And suddenly one hand was gripping a clump of grass and he was hauling himself over the lip of the cliff, sprawling and gasping on the damp floor of the bush.

When he stood up, the trees swung in a circle around him. Rob held to a tree-trunk till his giddiness stopped. He leaned forward till he could peer over the cliff, the thought of falling never entering his mind.

Down below he could make out a shape of blue and yellow that he knew was Shawn's jacket and his parka. There was no movement.

"You'll be OK, mate." Rob had no idea whether he spoke aloud or not. "I'll get help. No worries." He turned away from the cliff and set off into the bush.

Shawn had been right. The ground above the cliffs was mainly flat. Mainly flat and mainly clear, with only a few fallen and half-rotten trees to block the way.

On one level, Rob's mind was as clear as glass. He had to keep parallel to the river, till the cliffs ended and he could get down to the water again. Sooner or later the river would lead him out into farmland. All he had to do was to keep walking. He had nothing to carry now, not even his pack. He would walk all day and all night if he needed to. When he looked at his watch, he was jolted to find it was still only 8.02 am.

He pushed through low bushes, stumbled on old decayed stumps, never noticed the leaves stinging his face, and the new cuts and scratches marking his legs. The thought of resting had vanished from his mind.

A voice was there instead. It's your fault, the voice was telling him. If you'd done the right thing and not gone rushing off when Carl heard the hunters, none of this would have happened. You broke basic rules of tramping—Keep Together; Sit And Wait. You're breaking more basics right now: you're not leaving signs; you've left an injured person alone.

Lara and Carl, the voice nagged. Lara and Carl and now Shawn: they got hurt because of you. Even Harvey's body, lying there alone: that's your fault, too.

Rob knew the voice wasn't being fair. There was more to it than that. He'd done some things right. He'd tell the voice that when he had time. But he was busy just now.

He stumbled over a root, and grabbed a nearby branch

to save himself from falling. He picked briefly at the splinter left sticking into the side of his hand, forgot about it, and went on.

Thirty-two

In front of Rob's eyes there was a hand. The hand had a wrist. The wrist had a digital watch. As Rob stared, the figures on the watch changed. 11.56 am.

It's my hand, Rob realised. It's pressed against a tree-trunk, and I'm leaning my forehead against it. I've stopped. I've stopped because . . . that's right, because I can't get down to the river.

If he tried hard enough, he could remember things. The ground had started to slope uphill. The noise of the river had got fainter. Each time he worked his way to the edge of the cliff and stared down, the white-green thread rushing between the boulders was further below him.

He remembered something else, too. The cliffs and the river had curved suddenly, and he'd been able to look out. Out across a jagged landscape of bush-choked ridges, scarred by slips the size of city blocks, where shattered trees lay tumbled. Through this wilderness, the river in its cliff-lined gorge wound for miles into the distance.

It'll take you a week to get out of this, the voice in his mind sneered.

That's all right, a second voice answered. Rob supposed it was his own voice, talking aloud. I'll just walk for a week, then. I might even get to Double-Bend Station, where we were supposed to finish the tramp. That'll show you.

He was walking again now. He must have been walking again for a while. (If you could call it walking — he seemed to be banging into things a lot.) His watch said 1.04 pm.
"I'll get help," he heard the second voice say. Yes, it was his own voice, and it was talking aloud. Rob felt pleased he'd worked this out by himself. That's a good idea, Rob, he told himself. That's a good idea. You get help.

At 2.25 pm, Rob fell over. It wasn't a big fall. His legs just seemed to fold up, and he found himself on all fours, staring at his hands among the dirt and leaves of the bush floor, seeing the dots pulsing on his watch dial.

I must have fallen before, he thought. That's why there's blood all over my knee.

Oh, and I must be thirsty, too. After all, I haven't had anything to drink since before Shawn fell. Must be careful about that. I could die of thirst if I'm not careful.

Again he said out loud, "I'll get help. No worries, Shawn — Lara — Carl. I'll get help." Yes, that was the right idea. He was going to get help.

There was something strange about the trees, Rob decided. I know, there aren't any trees. That's why it's strange. And I've fallen over again.

There was tussock grass around him. Springy tussock grass, and a clear area half as big as a football field.

Dad and I sometimes find these clear bits when we go tramping, Rob remembered. What'd Dad say — a place where a couple of big trees fall, or where the wind blows too hard down the ridges for anything to grow except tussock. Good soft tussock, too. I could have a rest here. No, no, I'm supposed to be getting help.

Rob swayed upright. He couldn't read his watch. The figures seemed to blur, then sharpen, then blur again before he could take them in.

But suddenly his mind was clear. I'm not going to make it. I'm finished. Sorry, everybody. I gave it my best shot. Hope someone finds you. Tell Dad . . .

He was cold. Cold before he had time to think about it. Wind was blasting around him, slamming at him, knocking him sideways. No wonder trees can't grow here, he thought. Must be one of those places where the wind really howls down the ridges, like Dad told me. Better get into the bush for shelter.

Rob tried to start his legs moving towards the trees. But the wind was thrashing at him stronger than ever, roaring and bellowing in his ears as he sank again to his knees.

And at the far end of the clearing, something huge and orange settled from the sky, rotors flailing, sending tree branches tossing, whipping the tussock into waves, raising storms of dust into the air.

A door in the fuselage crashed open, and a figure was racing across the ground towards Rob, shouting, yelling his name. Another figure was dropping from the doorway and following. From the cockpit of the Sea-Eagle helicopter, a helmeted face stared through perspex in Rob's direction.

Then arms were around him, and his father's voice was laughing and sobbing in Rob's ears.

"Rob! Rob! We found your pack downstream. We've been searching the river valley. The other chopper — it's found the boy with the broken arm. They've got a medic with him."

The second man had arrived, and was standing grinning at the two of them. Rob's father was hugging Rob so hard that Rob could feel his arms going numb, and still shouting above the thwack and thunder of the helicopter. "Didn't know what had happened to the rest of you. Just climbing for a sweep when we saw something move in the clearing. Oh, Rob, Rob—I thought you were dead!"

Thirty-three

He was inside the helicopter, wrapped in a thermal blanket. His father had an arm around him so tightly that Rob couldn't see why they'd bothered doing up the shoulder belts and lap belts.

He held a bottle of glucose drink in his hands, and sipped occasionally from the built-in plastic straw. Funny thing was, the more he sipped, the thirstier he felt. His body seemed to be waking up again. His legs ached and shook; his hands were raw with cuts and scratches; his head felt thick and heavy.

There was something he had to tell his father. He turned his head painfully, and saw that his Dad was crying. Tears were gathering and running on his cheeks. But behind the tears, he was smiling at Rob.

"Oh, son—" His father stopped and tried again. "Son, if I'd lost you, too—"

"Dad," Rob said in turn. "I—Harvey—"

"We know about Harvey." Rob stared at his father in disbelief. "The other chopper found the remains of your fire about three hours back. They over-flew the same area yesterday morning, but they couldn't see anything in the rain. A couple of guys winched down—found Harvey's body and your other gear. That was a fine idea, Rob, laying him next to the tree like that."

Rob tried to shake his head, but it hurt too much.

"Dad — I messed things up. I didn't — "

His father stopped him. "Don't worry, son. You're safe. Nothing else matters."

Rob fell silent. Later he'd say what he'd done wrong. What he'd done wrong on the tramp and in the weeks before the tramp. Later. His Dad was right — they were safe; between them, nothing else mattered.

They waited on the ground for a few minutes, till the radio crackled and the pilot announced, "Other chopper's on its way to base. Patient's OK — broken arm and possible concussion, but nothing major. Now you can show us where the others are, young Rob."

The beat of the rotors quickened. Dust swirled around them. Then they were above the treetops, swinging up into the brilliant blue afternoon.

It had taken nearly thirty hours for Rob and Shawn, and then just Rob, to cover the distance from the slope of toi-toi where they'd left the others to the clearing where the helicopter found Rob. It took about five minutes to fly it.

"Is that the place?" asked Phil — the man who'd followed his father out of the chopper — impossibly soon. Then he and the pilot exclaimed together, "I see them!"

Three figures stood beside the big V and X laid out on the ground, frantically waving huge white hands. No, they were holding white toi-toi plumes and waving them, Rob realised. They look like those guys who signal to planes landing on aircraft carriers, he thought. Pity they're all waving in different directions.

Phil straightened up from examining Lara. The fair-haired girl still lay without moving in the stained sleeping-bag. Her face was the same grey-white colour. Phil's own face was grim. "Hospital as fast as possible for this one," he muttered, so only Rob's Dad and Rob heard him. "She's not too good at all."

Inside three minutes, Lara was lifted aboard the Sea-Eagle, strapped to a stretcher. Carl came aboard too, holding his sore side. "Thanks, Rob. Thanks, mate," he mumbled. He sank into a seat and closed his eyes.

There wasn't room for everyone, so Phil stayed on the ground with Wiki and Helen. Both girls hugged Rob and thanked him. Helen, when she heard that Shawn was hurt but OK, looked scared but relieved. Wiki, when she realised who Rob's father was, hugged Rob again and said "Told you so". Rob would have to tell her and Helen the truth about what had happened, too. Later.

"Other chopper'll be here in about five minutes," Phil was telling Wiki and Helen. "Try not to worry about Lara — we'll get her all the help we can. Now, who wants the Fruit-and-Nut, and who wants the Milky Bar?"

As Rob climbed back into the Sea-Eagle with his Dad, he heard Helen reply, "Doesn't matter. Wiki'll lose hers, anyway."

Search and Rescue Base was the Park Lodge where the six of them and Harvey had started off . . . six days ago? . . . seven days ago? Rob's mind couldn't work it out. The parking area was crammed with cars and people. An ambulance stood with its back doors open, lights flashing.

Rob staggered as he stepped down from the chopper, but his father's arm was around him again, holding him up. A woman was crying and calling Lara's name as the still figure on its stretcher was carried to the ambulance. Rob glimpsed a second stretcher already inside, which he guessed was Shawn. Another woman threw her arms around Carl, who gave a yelp of pain. Now this woman was crying too, and kissing the embarrassed boy.

Television cameras pushed at Rob. "How do you feel?" voices asked. "What was the worst part? Were you frightened at all?"

His father lifted his voice. "Please. He's asleep on his feet. He'll talk to you later. Leave him for a while, please."

One woman kept coming forward. Rob recognised the driver of the car that had dropped Shawn off, all those days before.

"Shawn says hi." The woman rested one hand on Rob's cheek. "And we both say thanks."

"I didn't — " Rob had things to explain to her, too, but she cut him off.

"You've given him a really good friend. He wants to know if you'll come and see him in hospital. You and Helen." The woman — Mrs Lander, Rob remembered now — smiled as she mentioned the tall girl's name.

The other chopper was touching down, and the TV cameras were hurrying towards it. Even through the perspex and the swirling dust, Rob could see Wiki's tired grin, and her hand holding a bar of chocolate. In spite of Lara, in spite of Harvey, in spite of everything in the last seven days, Rob grinned back.

"Let's find a place to sit and be quiet, eh, son?" Rob felt the arm around his shoulders start to tremble, and realised his father's voice was shaky too.

He grinned again. It was a wobbly, stupid grin, and he didn't know how he was going to get it off his face. But it was a grin all the same.

"OK, Dad," he mumbled. "Good thinking. Let's—let's take it easy."

SUNDAY: 11 JANUARY, 4.42 pm.

Base to Ground Parties: Choppers have got them all. The ambulance crews are taking over. You can start heading back now, guys and gals. Thanks heaps. Out.